# A GAME OF STRIP POKER

Miriam laughed and dealt the cards. He won. The second shoe slid off. Quite a few hands later, they were each down to their undies. Hers were white and lacy and matched the bra she'd had on. His were SpongeBob boxers his mother had bought him for Christmas.

"Really?" she said when she saw them.

"A joke from my mom. I wasn't thinking fast enough. I should have worn my Star Wars pair. They're sexier."

She dealt, picked up her cards, and smirked. Damn! Did the woman always win? He picked up his cards and leveled a look her way. "Bring it on," he said.

She spread out a flush, king high. He couldn't help the look of triumph on his face. He spread out a royal flush, ace high. "Remove the panties." His voice sounded hoarse.

She stood, all six feet of smooth, supple skin, put her fingers under her lacy skimp of fabric, and wriggled out of them. His heart clutched, stopped in his chest. He took a sharp breath. When was the last time he'd seen a naked woman?

"Damn, you're beautiful."

She rolled her eyes. "You've played mommy too long."

She had a point. He got a sudden case of nerves. "What now?"

"If you don't drop your drawers and screw me, I'm going to be disappointed."

"I wouldn't want that to happen."

She motioned to a room off the hallway. "My bedroom's in there . . ."

**Books by Judi Lynn**

COOKING UP TROUBLE
OPPOSITES DISTRACT
LOVE ON TAP
SPICING THINGS UP
FIRST KISS, ON THE HOUSE

**Published by Kensington Publishing Corporation**

# First Kiss,
# On the House

Judi Lynn

LYRICAL SHINE
Kensington Publishing Corp.
www.kensingtonbooks.com

LYRICAL SHINE BOOKS are published by

Kensington Publishing Corp.
119 West 40th Street
New York, NY 10018

First Electronic Edition: June 2017
eISBN-13: 978-1-5161-0137-5
eISBN-10: 1-5161-0137-5

First Print Edition: June 2017
ISBN-13: 978-1-5161-00138-2
ISBN-10: 1-5161-0138-3

Printed in the United States of America

# Chapter 1

Miriam Reinhardt rested her elbows on the bar and slumped forward on her stool.

Chase, the bar's owner, quirked an eyebrow at her. "That bad?"

"What can I say?" She reached for her purse and pushed a ten-dollar bill toward him. "It's the beginning of May. My students can smell the last day of school in their future. They get distracted if a breeze blows through the windows."

"How many years have you taught?"

"Forever."

"You're not old enough for that, but it's been long enough to know the drill." He grinned, and even after all these years, Miriam admired his good looks and easy charm.

"What will it be?" He picked up a mug.

"Hemlock on the rocks."

"Out of it at the moment. Your usual?"

"Beer fortifies me. Make it a double." She looked up as Tyne and Daphne walked through the door. Tyne didn't work on Monday nights, so they came to flank her, each taking one side and leaning in to hear about her day. They were so freaking happy since they'd gotten married, it almost made her teeth hurt.

Tyne narrowed his eyes, studying her. The man could dazzle at a thousand paces. So could Chase, who came to deliver a glass of wine to Daphne and mugs for her and Tyne. How in the hell had she chosen such attractive friends? It made her tall, gawky awkwardness all the more noticeable. Not that it mattered. Everyone in Mill Pond was used to her dark, corkscrew curls and endless boniness. They didn't give her a second glance, but a man she didn't know at a nearby booth kept staring at her. It was getting on her last nerve.

"Don't the kids call you Drill Sergeant Reinhardt?" Tyne asked. "I'd lay money you keep them working till the last minute of the last day of high school."

She couldn't deny that. "They all know my reputation. I expect their best and they'd damn well better deliver it."

Daphne sipped her wine, then asked, "The end of the year's when you hit them with your big guns, isn't it? What have you got them doing now?"

"Comparing how three different writers of their choice deal with a social issue in their novels."

"Say again?" Tyne reached for a bowl of popcorn and drew it toward them.

Miriam tried to explain. "They pick a topic. Maya—"

Tyne interrupted. "Our Maya? The girl who lives with Paula's mom at the inn and helps babysit for the employees with kids?"

Miriam nodded. "A superbrain. She chose women's roles in society. She's reading *Pride and Prejudice*, Germaine Greer's *The Female Eunuch*, and *The Handmaid's Tale* by Margaret Atwood."

Tyne stared. "You know this is high school, right?"

"It's my advanced English class. I expect more. Greg Lewis plans to study public finance in college. He chose *The Wolf of Wall Street*, *The Grapes of Wrath*, and *Nothin' But Blue Skies* by Edward McClelland."

Chase had a break between customers and came over to listen. He gave a low whistle. "How many pages do their papers have to be?"

"Ten, but they get to work on them during class and ask for feedback."

Daphne took another handful of popcorn. Miriam's best friend had gained a few pounds after marrying Tyne, but they looked good on her. "That's only for your advanced class, right?"

"My two regular classes only have to read one book and report on its theme." She took another swig of her beer and looked up to see the man at the booth openly staring at her again. He didn't even have the decency to look away when she caught him at it. What was she? Some kind of freak show for his entertainment? Irritated, she snapped, "What are you looking at?"

The man grabbed his beer, gave a big smile, and rose to join them at the bar.

What the hell? Before she could blurt out something rude, Daphne interrupted. "I should have introduced you. Joel Worth, this is my friend, Miriam, and my husband, Tyne. Joel's renting the apartment above my stained-glass shop until he can find some place permanent to stay. He came to Mill Pond to start a microbrewery."

Chase's aquamarine eyes sparkled with interest. He reached across the bar to shake Joel's hand. "It's about time we had local beers to serve around here. Are you opening a bar?"

He didn't sound a bit concerned about competition. Why would he? When Miriam came for a burger and beer in the summer, she had to come early to find a seat. So many tourists visited Mill Pond during peak season that there'd be enough business for both him and Joel.

Joel grimaced and shook his head. "Not a true bar. Too much work. I noticed there's no hot dog stand around here. I'm going to serve brews and dogs."

Chase licked his lips. "I love a good dog."

"Finished on a griddle, right?" As a chef, Tyne took food prep seriously. Miriam had been invited to enough dinners at Daphne's to appreciate his skills.

"Yup. I've already ordered the flattop and a steamer for the buns. I have a good Coney sauce recipe, but I'm still tinkering with that."

Tyne's brown eyes sparkled. "Maybe I can help you."

When Joel frowned, Daphne explained, "He's a chef. He knows food."

"For free? The last chef I asked wanted a bundle for his expertise."

"This is Mill Pond," Tyne said. "Neighbors help each other."

"Even if my place is on the edge of town?"

"You're looking at the old dairy, right?" Chase asked. "That's a good location, close enough that tourists will drop in."

"Iris Clinger is taking me there for one last look-see tomorrow." He shrugged. "Or did you already know that, too?"

Daphne shook her head. "Get used to it. This is Mill Pond. Everyone knows everyone else's business."

Chase refilled Miriam's mug. "Anyone who lives around here is a neighbor. It takes new people a while to get used to us, but we pitch in if we can."

"And you?" Joel's gaze turned to Miriam. "Do you own a shop in town?"

"Not me. I'm a lowly English teacher." She took another gulp of beer.

He locked gazes with her. "I always had crushes on my teachers. I like smart women."

*Yeah right.* Every kid fell for their first-grade teacher. Not that many were enamored of the high school teacher from hell. Miriam glanced at Joel's left hand. No ring. But some men didn't wear their wedding bands.

He caught her looking and smiled. "You're single, too?"

"Yup, the town's official old maid schoolmarm."

"For a schoolmarm, you seem to really like beer."

He had her there. "I'm not classy enough for wine. More of a broad, if you know what I mean."

"Do you like sports?"

She wrinkled her nose. For her, the two didn't necessarily go together. "I'd rather watch *Pride and Prejudice.*"

"I can do that, too."

*Was he hitting on her? How desperate was this man?* He was pleasant enough to look at, five ten with limp, sandy-brown hair and gray eyes. Not a hottie like Tyne or Chase. Just nice. He had a little belly on him, not the rock-hard abs they had. Miriam liked bellies— a soft pillow to rest your head on.

Miriam raised her eyebrow—her school teacher intimidation tactic. "Be warned, Daphne's new friend. I have an acid tongue."

"And a great laugh. They balance each other, don't you think?"

*What was with this guy?* He hardly knew her. He must not have gotten laid for a long time and was looking for a quick thrill. That was fine with her. He was nothing special, but then, neither was she.

She'd never been good at coy, so she decided to be direct. "I'm too busy for any distractions until school's out. I'm going to be buried in term papers."

"Works for me. I'm a patient man." He drained his glass and gave her a wink. "I'm setting up my brewery. I'll be busy, too, but whenever you want me to make time for you, let me know." He put money on the bar and nodded at the others. "Nice meeting all of you."

Miriam stared as he walked out the door. Then, she asked, "Do you think he's for real?"

Tyne and Chase grinned in unison. Tyne's brown eyes glittered with amusement. "I think you've got yourself a contender, Drill Sergeant."

# Chapter 2

Joel gave his daughter, Adele, a kiss on the cheek before he left for the day. "What do you have planned while I'm gone?"

She grinned. "I'm going to watch old movies on the Hallmark Channel. You got the internet connected yesterday, didn't you?"

He switched on the TV and flipped to the right station. He didn't like to leave Adele alone in front of the TV, but he'd kept her busy the last few days, unpacking and getting the kitchen and bedrooms ready to live in. They hadn't unpacked anything but the basics, but they could manage here until they found someplace better. "Do you have everything you need for snacks and lunch?"

She nodded, impatient for him to leave. "There's plenty of deli meat in the refrigerator for sandwiches and you bought yogurt and hummus and a cupboard full of chips."

"If you need anything . . ."

She interrupted him. "Daphne's downstairs in her stained-glass shop."

Joel felt torn. He'd talked to Daphne about Adele and she'd volunteered to be backup if he needed her. She knew Adele would be alone today and had agreed to check on her between customers. He'd left Adele before and she was fine, but he always worried. She was nineteen but had been born with cerebral palsy. His blond, pretty daughter would be mentally twelve for the rest of her life. He'd trained her over and over again not to answer the door when he was gone and never to use the stove, and she'd always followed his instructions. Usually, she just sat in front of the TV and lost herself in show after show. That was why he only left her on her own when he couldn't think of some other arrangement.

A car honked at the curb and Joel grinned. "Enjoy yourself. Be safe." Then he ran down the stairs and out the door to slide into Iris Clinger's car. "Can we finalize the deal today?" he asked.

Iris gave her pleasant smile. Close to sixty, she was a little on the plump side with red hair that had faded to sandy-colored. She had warm brown eyes and laugh lines. "If you like it, it's yours. All you have to do is sign the contract."

Relief flowed through him. He'd made the right choice moving to Mill Pond for a fresh start. He'd bought and fixed up enough strip malls that when he'd sold them all, he'd have a secure future whether the microbrewery made much money or not. At thirty-seven, he could try something fun, and he'd always wanted to make beer.

Iris drove him to the old dairy on the southeast edge of town. The long, low building had an office near the front door. The place was big enough to suit his needs, and it sat on enough property to put a trailer near the trees in back.

Iris waved a hand. "Well? What do you think?"

"This will work." There'd be enough room for a dining area and a family room besides the brewery, and it would be easy to add a patio outside.

She gave him a sideways glance. "Do you think your wife will like Mill Pond?"

Joel bit back a smile. Iris knew he had a daughter. She was trying to find out if he was married. "I hope not. That's why I'm moving, to get away from my ex."

Iris lit up. She must consider herself a matchmaker. "We have a lot of pretty girls in Mill Pond."

"Most of them would run from me."

"You're selling yourself short." Iris looked him up and down. "You seem especially nice to me."

"I try to be, but my daughter's nineteen. She can't use her right side very well and she'll always be mentally challenged. Most women don't want to take on a kid who'll never be able to leave the nest."

Iris's expression melted with sympathy. "Her mother doesn't help?"

Joel shrugged. "My ex-wife is fragile, troubled, couldn't deal with Adele. Can barely cope herself."

"You poor man."

"I've stopped thinking of myself that way. I thank the heavens every day for Adele." Okay, his marriage had been a bust, but April had given him Adele. He'd married her with the idea of rescuing her, but he'd been young. There were some things you couldn't fix. He hadn't realized the odds were too stacked against him. Then Adele had been born with problems, but how many parents had such a sweet, generous child? True, she'd *always* be a child, but there was some beauty in that, right?

Iris hesitated. "Mill Pond is a close, giving community. Adele will be well-treated here."

The same thing people had said at the bar the night before. After his conversation with them, he'd realized anything and everything he told Iris today would be known all over Mill Pond by morning, but he was okay with that. People might as well know all his dirty laundry. Then it would be out there, in the open. "I'm hoping to put a trailer on the back of the property close to the trees."

Iris frowned. "But there are plenty of nice houses and cabins for sale."

"I know, but eventually, I'll probably end up with my brother, Miles." Might as well spill the beans now and get it over with. "He's an alcoholic who's struggling to get himself together. I'd like to hire him as a custodian for the brewery and let him live on site."

Iris took a deep breath. "Are you going to take in every troubled person you can?"

"Nope, I've learned my limits. Only family, and Adele and Miles are more than enough for me."

She placed a hand on his arm. "I've lived longer than you have. Take care of yourself or taking care of others will drain you, leave you empty. You won't have anything to offer, not for them, not for yourself."

He appreciated her honesty. "That's why I left my ex. I understand what you're telling me."

Her shoulders relaxed. She'd been worried about him. That was nice. "So, do you want to sign the contract?" she asked.

Once their business was over, she drove him back to town. On the way, he thought about their conversation. He'd grown up with Miles. He recognized a troubled person when he saw one, so why had he gotten April pregnant when they were seniors in high school? Because he was young and stupid and she was so needy, he'd wanted to make her feel loved. Talk about naïve.

Never again. If he ever fell in love again, it would be with some-one sturdy and solid. An Amazon.

He thought of Miriam. The woman looked like she could give as good as she got. A challenge.

He pushed her out of his mind and turned to Iris. "Are there any outlets around here you think would be good for my product?"

"Honey, you've come to the right place." She turned at Lake Drive. They passed farms on the far side of the road and the marina and public beaches on the other. "You need to meet Ian McGregor. He runs the resort on the lake and his wife owns the bakery and farm stand next door."

She parked in the lot of a sprawling inn with the lake at its back. It of-fered tennis courts, a golf course, and horse stables. Joel was impressed. She led him inside and a tall man with dark hair and chocolate-brown eyes circled the check-in counter to greet him.

"Joel, this is Ian," Iris said by way of introduction.

Ian extended a hand. "Tyne told me about you."

Tyne popped his head out of the office when he heard his name and grinned when he recognized Joel. "The beer maker! Nice to see you again." He followed Ian to greet him. "I've been tinkering with Coney recipes."

Joel blinked his surprise. He'd been worried he'd be odd man out in a small town, that longtime residents would be cliquey. Instead, he'd been greeted with open arms. Not what he'd expected. "I asked Iris about possible markets for my beer and she brought me here." Joel had researched Mill Pond, but he hadn't thought of selling beer to the inn.

Ian gestured him toward the inn's dining room. "A good thing. We buy all our wine from Harley's winery, but we've never offered beer. We try to avoid name brands to support local farmers and sup-pliers. Once you get up and running, stop by to talk to me."

"Will do." Joel's gaze roamed to the wide expanse of windows at the back of the room. The view of the lake was stunning.

"You need to meet Mill Pond's farmers and suppliers," Tyne told him. "I work night shifts, so I can drive you around and introduce you to them. I have tomorrow open. What do you say?"

"Who could turn that down?" Joel shook his head. "You people sure are friendly. I was worried it would take me twentysome years to fit in here."

Ian laughed. "Mill Pond's trying to grow, to attract more tourists. Every businessman wants the next one to succeed. That way we can offer more, draw in more people."

It made sense. These people worked together instead of competing. Joel felt himself relax more. He might not only make it here but he was sure to enjoy the new people he'd meet.

# Chapter 3

Miriam propped her hip on her desk corner and studied her advanced students. "I've brought in a guest speaker today. Thought you might need a break from your projects." Actually, she'd brought in a speaker for all her three of her English classes. She taught journalism, too, but most of those students were already in one of her other classes.

"Our guest isn't here just to talk about colleges. I know not every kid—not even the smart ones—likes school. I don't care if you go on to a trade school, a two-year program, or a prestigious college, as long as you use your potential and follow your passions."

The class looked relieved to forget their research papers for a day. They glanced at the speaker expectantly.

Miriam motioned to the woman waiting to be introduced. "I've invited Leticia Grayston to speak with you today. Most of you already have applied to and maybe even been accepted by universities, but not all of you have made up your minds. Leticia is a therapist and I deeply respect her work. She's here to talk about how to develop the best of who you are. Enjoy her presentation."

Miriam settled behind her desk to watch her students while Leticia spoke. The therapist grabbed their attention immediately, as Miriam knew she would. Leticia talked about accepting who you were, your strengths and foibles, liking yourself, staying true to yourself, and reaching your potential. These kids were motivated. They hung on her words.

Before she realized it, Miriam found herself watching Maya's reactions. Maya was in Miriam's journalism class, too. She'd come to her for help applying for scholarships.

"I don't know where to start," she'd told her. "My parents won't help me because they disowned me. I don't want to graduate with tons of debt."

Miriam had dug in with enthusiasm. Maya had to have a shot for a free ride in college. She was a superbrain and had worked hard for top grades. At one time, Miriam had worried that the girl wouldn't make it out of Mill Pond. Her family seemed determined to doom her to a life of low wages, but then Maya's stepfather had made a move on her, and that made Maya's mother jealous, and the girl had gotten tossed out of her home through no fault of her own.

*The best thing that could ever happen to her.* Miriam had been delighted when Paula's mother had taken her in to help run the day care in Ian's inn. The security had made the girl blossom.

Maya was listening with rapt attention, but Miriam wondered what message she was hearing. She wished Leticia would say, *And stay away from boys. They're nothing but a distraction at your age. Don't go there.*

Maya had been in line for some serious scholarships, but lately, she didn't seem as driven as usual. She'd been spending a lot of time with T. J. Preston, a nice enough boy and certainly good-looking but not very focused. Miriam worried she'd rather hook up with him and take a low-paying job to stay in Mill Pond. *Don't do it!* Miriam screamed inside her head. But kids rarely heard telepathy, so she hoped Leticia's lecture would help.

When the speech was over and the kids filed out of the room, Leticia raised her eyebrows at Miriam. Last year Leticia had worked with one of Miriam's students who'd tried to commit suicide. She'd turned the girl around. "Well? What do you think? Did your girl take any of it in?"

"She listened well enough."

Leticia shook her head sadly. "Not the same as hearing."

"God, I know. I just hate to see a kid throw away her future. I hope some of it sank in."

Leticia came close and patted her arm. "If there's one thing I've learned in my profession, it's that you can do your best to inspire and nurture but you can't win 'em all."

"Amen to that." Still, Miriam couldn't help herself from giving it her best try. She had speakers set up for her two other classes, too, people who worked at employment agencies, to talk about what businesses wanted and how to succeed in the work world. College or not, she wanted her students to do well.

Leticia hugged her good-bye. "You've done your best. Now it's up to them."

They were eighteen-years-old. What did they know? But today would make them think. And as a personal bonus, with speakers, Miriam wouldn't have papers to grade tonight. She might even get caught up if she hit it hard when she got home.

She was feeling pretty upbeat when the last bell rang and the kids flew out of the building. She stayed for a half hour more, working on lesson plans, before she headed to the parking lot. And there, near the back of the lot, was a black Chevy, with Maya pressed against it in a tight embrace with T. J., their lips locked.

Damn it all to hell! Miriam had to stop herself from marching back there and yanking them apart. What was Maya thinking? Wait . . . did she really want to know? A chill made the hairs on her arms stand on end when T. J.'s hands slid under Maya's blouse.

The girl was too young, not savvy enough. What to do? She called and waved. "Have a great night, kids!"

They jerked apart. Maya's face flushed fiery red. Good, she was embarrassed. She should be. Would she stop making out with T. J.? Hell no. With no affection at home, she'd found it elsewhere.

Now Miriam was really worried. Her thoughts turned away from which college Maya should choose to whether the girl knew about birth control and if she was being careful. It was time to pull her aside and give her the *lecture*. Hell, she'd buy her condoms if Maya would let her, pay for her to be on the Pill or, even better, the Shot.

With a new plan in mind, Miriam slid behind the steering wheel of her car and started for home. Driving down Main Street always lifted her spirits with its old-fashioned streetlamps and striped window canopies. Every flower box and keg already brimmed with blooms.

She gave a rueful laugh as she passed Art's Grocery store, Grams's church, and Daphne's stained-glass shop. She had condoms waiting in her nightstand at home, but they'd been there so long, they'd probably withered with age by now. Same could be said for her. She'd been ready a long time, but there hadn't been any takers.

Maya had found a taker, though. And that changed things. If the girl didn't go to college this fall, she could go later, if she didn't get pregnant. Babies made everything more complicated. Time to spell things out for her.

# Chapter 4

Joel watched Tyne's bright orange Jeep pull to the curb in front of Daphne's shop the next morning. When Tyne noticed him, he grinned and beckoned him with a wave.

"Oh boy." The top was off, the windows gone. Joel reached for his heavy jacket. He didn't own black leather like Tyne wore. He'd be the uncool passenger, trying not to freeze to death because early May wasn't warm enough for whizzing around town in the open air.

Adele came to glance out the window, too. When she saw Tyne, her jaw dropped.

"He's married," Joel warned. His daughter had watched too many movies with Prince Charmings of one kind or another, and Tyne sure looked the part—if Disney ever showed princes with scruffy chins and way too much sex appeal. She'd never met anyone like him.

Steps pounded up the stairs before Joel finished his list of reminders to his daughter. "And if you need anything . . ."

". . . Daphne's downstairs," Adele finished for him.

Tyne knocked, then cracked open the door. "You ready?"

Joel should have figured Tyne was a doer, not good at waiting, the type who plunged into things instead of dipping his toes in the water. Joel had learned patience from his daughter. Her right foot was slightly turned in, so she couldn't walk fast. Her right hand was twisted, too, so it took her a while to open mail or cut her food. At first, he'd pulled her plate over and done it for her, but then he'd realized he wasn't helping her by *helping* her. She was better off doing as many things as she could on her own.

Adele gazed at Tyne, a dazed expression on her face and her hand over her heart.

Joel motioned him inside and nodded toward her. "Tyne, this is my daughter, Adele."

Tyne's glance flicked over her deformed right side. He gave a dazzling smile. "Nice to meet you."

Adele bit her bottom lip, suddenly shy.

Tyne took it in his stride. Joel had the feeling women more often than not tripped over themselves when they met him. "I came to show your dad around town and introduce him to some people in the business. Do you hold down the fort while he's gone?"

She blushed fiery red all the way to her hairline. "I watch TV."

"Good enough; you're on call if he needs you."

That made her smile, and Joel knew they'd be leaving her happy. "Take care, kiddo. See you later." He followed Tyne down the steps and climbed into the Jeep next to him.

"Nice kid," Tyne said.

Joel squinted at him to see if he was serious. Most people who met Adele made comments or asked questions. "She has cerebral palsy."

"She's still a nice kid."

Joel laughed. How refreshing! "That she is."

"I thought I'd drive you around town first, show you the layout, and then introduce you to a few people."

"Works for me." Joel grabbed the door handle as Tyne jerked into gear. Then he held on for good measure as Tyne sped down Main Street and turned toward the nearby national forest.

"The forest is what brings so many tourists to town," Tyne explained. "They stop at Mill Pond on the way to the nature trails and lodges." They sped past corn and wheat fields until he pointed to a log cabin with a green tin roof about twenty minutes from town. The forest served as its backyard. "That's our place. Daphne bought it years ago; lucky for me. I love nature."

He turned right at the next road and headed toward the water. When they reached Lake Drive, he turned right again and took Joel to Harley's winery. "You'll like Harley. He, Chase, and I go biking together in the summer."

"Biking? No wonder you're in such good shape." Joel wondered how many miles they rode.

"Motorcycles," Tyne said, ruining that idea. He drove to a large white stucco building with a sign that announced TASTING ROOM. At least a dozen other cars were in the lot. "Come on."

A tall man with dark, shaggy hair and five o'clock stubble walked toward them before they were inside. "I've been helping over at Dad's new place, saw you pull in."

Tyne turned to look at a long, low-slung ranch house with a tiled roof on the other side of the tasting room. "How's it coming? It looks done."

"They're landscaping today, moving in furniture tomorrow. Dad and Vicki can hardly wait." The stucco house was painted white to match the original house on the other side of the property. Harley turned to Joel. "My dad was a widower. He just remarried. He's pretty excited about starting over."

Fresh starts. New beginnings. "That's why I'm moving here," Joel admitted. "I get it."

Harley stretched out a hand. "Our introductions got a little neglected. I'm Harley. You must be the new brew guy."

"Joel Worth." He felt odd, sandwiched between the two tall, gorgeous men. Weren't there any ordinary guys in Mill Pond? They didn't seem to think a thing about it, though. Maybe if he stood on a stool, he'd feel more secure. He'd never felt short before, just average. This was a new sensation. Come to think of it, though, he hadn't felt short when he stood next to Miriam, and she had him by a couple of inches, too. He cleared his throat to answer. "I bought the old dairy on the southeast side of town. Mean to make it into a hot dog place and microbrewery."

"I'm addicted to Chicago dogs." Harley grinned his approval. "Fell in love with them when I took Kathy there a year ago. Don't suppose you'll offer those?"

"Sure will. I want some variety. Coneys. Chicago dogs. Big Apple–style with spicy mustard and sauerkraut. I have ten different topping choices on my menu."

"You've done it now." Harley laughed. "Kathy, my wife, is going to love your place. My dad gets a little gung ho about Italian. She likes a break once in a while."

Joel watched as another car parked near the tasting room and four people walked inside. "Is it busy around here this time of year?"

Harley glanced in the windows at the people crowding around the tasting bar. "Busy enough. Peak season starts when the kids get out of school, but plenty of adults come before it gets so crowded."

"Once it's warm weather?" Joel asked.

Tyne shook his head. "You'll be surprised how long our tourist season lasts. The big months are June, July, and August, but a lot of people come to see the leaves change in October. They come for specialty items for Thanksgiving and Christmas. Plus, the town goes all out, decorating for the holidays. It doesn't really get slow until January, and then it picks up again as soon as the weather gets better in spring. Sometimes that's as early as March."

"That's better than I thought." Joel had expected a longer downtime.

"Some people come just to get away for a long weekend," Harley said. "If the roads are decent, they make the trip. And now that Ian's started offering special weekend packages for holidays, they even come for Valentine's Day."

Tyne glanced at his watch. "Hate to say it, but we'd better go. I'm giving him the grand tour today and you're only our first stop. See you later, Harley."

Harley glanced at his watch. "You'd better set a timer. People in Mill Pond love to talk about our town."

Joel was getting that idea. "Where to next?" he asked Tyne as they pulled away.

"Thought I'd take you to the farmers close to Ian's inn. They all raise specialty goods. They won't be markets for your beer, but they're good to know. And then I'll finish with Art's Grocery. He loves to feature local products. Has a special room for them. It's one of the biggest draws in his store for tourists."

More time passed than Joel expected. Harley was right. Every farmer wanted to talk about his product and the town. David Danza and his wife, Darinda, raised a variety of fowl on their farm—chickens, guinea hens, ducks, geese, pheasants. Darinda was a teacher, so she wasn't home when they stopped by, but that just gave David more time to explain how his farm was run. The Albertsons had a dairy herd and the Kruses raised corn, soybeans, and wheat.

"I'd take you off the main roads, but we'd never get home," Tyne told him. "Carl Gruber lives down that road, and he raises grass-fed beef." He pointed down another road. "Evan Meyers breeds goats, and he and his sons produce cheese."

Joel tried to remember the names but knew it was impossible. The wind whipped his cheeks to the same rosy red as Tyne's as they zipped toward town. He was relieved when they finally stopped at Art's Grocery.

Art left his small office to greet Tyne when they stepped inside. A young man and a young woman worked two cash registers, and they looked a lot like Art, with dark hair and dark eyes. All three had stocky builds. The son had his dad's wide face and friendly smile.

"Hey, didn't expect to see you today." Art clapped Tyne on the back. "Thought you stocked up yesterday."

"I did, but I came to introduce you to Joel Worth. He's going to open a microbrewery at the old dairy."

"Ah, you're the one! Glad Tyne brought you in. I stock local specialties in our Hometown Room. We added a wing onto the store for it. Come on. I'll show you."

When they walked through the arch, it felt like they were entering an old-time store. Art had installed an oak-plank floor and wooden barrels, filled with different flavored taffy and candies, clustered around tables displaying breads and desserts. Joel's eyes widened in surprise. A long meat counter sold the Danzas' chickens and fowls, as well as Carl Gruber's beef. Harley's wine and a local orchard's cider took up one corner, and Evan Meyers's cheeses another. There were jars of homegrown honey, apple butters, and all kinds of fresh produce.

"We get the produce from Ian's wife, Tessa. She sells it at her farm stand, too," Art explained. He smiled at Joel. "I'd sure love to stock some specialty beers."

They talked business for a while before Tyne tapped his watch. "Sorry, but I'm running out of time. I work the supper shift tonight. We've got to go."

It was a short drive to Daphne's stained-glass shop, and when Joel took the stairs to his apartment to check on Adele, Tyne ducked into the shop to see his wife. Joel watched as Daphne looked up to see Tyne, her whole face lighting up. A short stab of pain zinged through him. Someday he'd like someone to look at him like that. And once again he thought of Miriam.

# Chapter 5

Miriam stopped to look around at all the customers as she walked into Chase's bar. She wasn't in need of liquid fortification tonight. She wanted to talk to Chase's wife, Paula, and luckily, she was sitting at the bar. Miriam slid on to the stool next to hers.

Paula eyed her warily. "You have that look, the serious one when you have something on your mind."

Miriam motioned for a beer. When Chase brought it, she said, "Can I order a burger, too?"

"It's better than drinking on an empty stomach." Chase winked at her. He liked to give her a hard time.

"Pickles, lettuce, tomato, and lots of mayo," she told him.

He slid his pencil back behind his ear and went to deliver her order.

Paula repeated her question. "What's up?"

"I was hoping you could do me a favor."

"Probably, if I can. I won't loan you Chase, though, and Daphne won't rent out Tyne."

Miriam laughed. "This is about hormones." She explained about seeing Maya in the school parking lot with T. J. "He had his hands under her blouse and she was liking it. Is she on birth control?"

Paula's expression changed. The proverbial lightbulb had turned on over her head as she got the idea. "I doubt it. My mom didn't know she was hooked up with a guy." Maya lived with Paula's mother in Ian's inn. Together, they babysat for Ian's employees, including Paula's kids before and after school. Her mom had wanted to keep Aiden and Bailey longer tonight or Paula would be upstairs in their apartment, playing mommy.

"Would your mom give her the birds-and-bees talk?" Miriam

asked. "I would, but the kids tune me out. They know I never get any, so I'm not a good source."

Paula grinned. "You're not that innocent. You've had a few guys."

"In college, nothing serious. If it's true if you don't use it, you lose it, my ovaries are history."

Paula had to press her hand over her mouth not to spurt out her last sip of beer. "You always make me laugh. It's not safe to drink around you."

Miriam turned serious again. "I think I've lost Maya for a while. She doesn't want to leave town to go to college."

"Hell, she could drive back and forth every day," Paula said. "Bloomington's that close."

"I'm trying, but her focus is on T. J. right now. I can deal with that. In a year or two she might change her mind, and then she can make the trip—if she doesn't have a kid to worry about."

Paula nodded. "I'll talk to Mom."

"I'll pay for the Pills. The Shot might be even better, if your mom can talk her into taking one or the other."

A car honked, and Paula looked out the glass doors. "There's Mom now with the kids. Gotta go and corral my hoodlums. I'll talk to her, though."

"Thanks." Miriam watched Paula go, and as her friend opened the doors to leave, Joel walked through them to enter. He saw Miriam, gave a small wave, and came to join her.

"Hi again," he said.

This time she really looked at him. He gave the impression of being a nice person, and tonight he looked bemused. She frowned at him. "Is everything okay?"

Her hamburger came and Joel's stomach rumbled. "Mind if I eat with you?"

"Go for it."

He ordered a bacon cheeseburger with sliced jalapeños. When Chase served his beer, Joel took a long swig. Then he let out a long sigh.

Miriam cocked an eyebrow. "Okay, you're starved and you're stunned. Which came first?"

He smiled. "I spent the day with Tyne, meeting suppliers and people around town."

"And Tyne forgot to stop for lunch." She'd seen Tyne in action. When the man focused on something, it got done, no matter what.

"We grabbed some cheese and crackers at Harley's, but I met everyone he could introduce me to. That was nice of him."

"Pretty Boy is at the top of my list, but he's a little obsessive."

"Pretty Boy?"

"My nickname for him. Everyone else calls him Hot Stuff. He calls me E.T. for English Teacher, and he named Paula Goth Girl."

"You must be close."

Miriam waited while Chase brought Joel his burger, then said, "He married my best friend. He's perfect for her and he feeds me when I pop by their place."

They both took a minute to bite into their burgers. When they moaned in unison, Joel actually blushed. Pretty sweet really. She narrowed her eyes at him. "Okay, so I know why you're starved. What's with the stunned look?"

He paused to choose his words carefully. "I have a daughter, Adele. She's nineteen, but she'll never grow up. Cerebral palsy. At home, my parents took care of her once in a while, so I could go out, do something fun." He stumbled for a minute. "Not that Adele isn't fun. It's just that . . ."

". . . once in a while you want to be around adults. Yeah, I get that."

His shoulders relaxed. "Anyway, I don't worry when I leave her during the day for a while. Daphne checks in on her when she can, and then I make sure I'm at home at night. Except tonight, Paula's mom came and invited her out for pizza."

Miriam nodded. "Hazel's great like that, loves kids."

"But she doesn't know Adele. She said Tyne told her about her and she wanted to meet her. That's never happened to us before."

Miriam reached for a fry. "You're in Mill Pond. Things are different here."

"How different?"

How could she describe it to him? Finally, she said, "People are nice to one another."

"That's what Iris said, but I thought that meant they smiled and waved." He looked thoughtful. "Adele was so happy, she almost cried."

Miriam felt for him. "It's tough raising a kid with special needs."

She hesitated, then asked what she was sure he'd been asked many times before, "Does her mother help?"

He shook his head. "April has enough problems of her own."

"Then Adele's better off not having her in her life."

Not everyone understood that, but it was true. "That's why we moved here." Joel finished his burger and nodded for a second beer. "April showed up on our doorstep every time she had a problem. When her car broke down. When she forgot to pay the rent. I don't mind helping her, but I asked her over and over again to just call me, not to stop by the house where Adele would see her. It upset Adele every time."

Miriam finished her burger, too, and turned to stare at him. "You don't mind helping your ex-wife?"

"It's complicated."

"You're a nice man." Miriam admired nice. Too many people took it for weakness. She didn't. "You set boundaries, right?"

"I have to. I like myself, too."

"See? I knew you were smart." She ordered a second beer and rested her elbows on the bar to yak with him while he finished his.

He took a long gulp, then wiped his lips with the back of his hand. "Enough talk about me. What about you? You're an English teacher. What else?"

She blinked. "That's about it. I don't cook. Suck at it. I spent a fortune on an AGA stove for my cottage on the lake, but that was only because I love Agatha Christie and wanted to pretend I'm British."

He laughed. "Good thing you don't want to be Elizabeth Bennet. She's fighting zombies right now."

"I know! I loved that movie."

That made him laugh harder. "What do you do in the summer when you don't teach?"

"I garden. I read. I row my boat out on the lake to fish."

"You fish?"

"I let them all go. I have two cats—Tommy and Tuppence."

"Agatha Christie again, right?"

She stared. "Have you read them?"

"No, but I watched the TV shows when they were on PBS or A&E, I can't remember which."

"You watch British mysteries?" She clinked her glass with his. "You're a good man."

"I can cook, too," he told her. "Nothing fancy like Tyne, but enough to keep Adele and me fed."

"What does Adele like? What are some of her favorite things?"

"Macaroni and cheese, chicken strips . . ."

She shook her head. "No, not food. What makes her happy?"

"She'd watch TV twenty-four hours a day if I let her. Has a thing for every Disney movie ever made. She loves the water. One of the other reasons I moved here. Someday I want to buy a boat."

The words popped out of her mouth before she could stop them. "You should bring her to my place on Saturday. We can order a pizza or something. I live on the lake." Then she wrinkled her nose in a grimace. "Don't look at the dust, though. If you have allergies, you might die."

He shook his head, amused. "That bad?"

"I dust once a month whether it needs it or not. I've been too busy lately, grading papers, so it's worse than usual."

"You sound like my kind of woman. My ex had OCD, cleaned all the time. If I sat a beer on the end table, she whisked it away before I could finish it."

His kind of woman. The words stuck in her mind. What would that be like? "Okay, if I haven't scared you away, bring Adele to my place for supper around six. Does that work for you?"

He grabbed her tab and added it to his, paying for both of them. "We'll be there."

She walked out of the bar with him and, on the drive home, let a bubble of excitement swell inside her. A man was coming to her cottage of his own free will. He was bringing his daughter with him, but so what? She liked kids. This might be the beginning of something nice—a male friend, even if he didn't come with benefits.

# Chapter 6

A boat went by in front of Miriam's cottage, waking her at nine on Saturday morning. She glanced at the light creeping past the edges of her blinds. No alarm clock. Heaven. Tommy, her gray tiger cat, was pressed against the back of her legs. Tuppence, the gray female with a white throat and paws, was curled near her stomach. She was sandwiched by cats. Could life get any better?

A second boat passed in the opposite direction. Sounded like a pontoon. An ordinance prevented ski boats from revving their engines until ten a.m. to give fishermen a chance to peacefully enjoy the lake in the early hours. Once ten hit, though, the temperatures rose and the lake became a playground for tubing and skis.

Miriam turned on her back to stretch. "Time to move it," she warned the cats. They knew the routine. The king-size bed took up most of the room, but it was worth it. At nearly six feet, Miriam didn't want her feet to dangle over the end of the mattress.

She pushed out of bed and opened the blinds to look at the lake. A beautiful day. A robin's-egg blue sky cradled puffy white clouds and the water sparkled as if filled with sunbeams.

She padded into the long, narrow kitchen and poured herself a cup of hot coffee. Agatha Christie would probably be ashamed of her and recommend tea, but Agatha was British. She hadn't enjoyed the kick of caffeine that strong java could give you. Then, dressed in long pajamas, Miriam opened the kitchen door and went on to the back patio that overlooked the lake while she sipped from her mug. The cats followed her, curling at her feet to greet the day. They sat out there, enjoying a slow start to their day, until ten o'clock hit and the first speedboat revved by the cottage.

"You hungry?" Miriam led the cats inside and filled their food bowls. Joel and his daughter were coming for supper tonight, and she thought about dusting before they got to her house but decided to grade papers instead. She opened the cupboards for sustenance to survive the weary task of pushing a red pen over page after page of term papers, but she hadn't gone to the store. There wasn't much to choose from. She ended up making herself three peanut butter sandwiches to stave off starvation and got down to business.

Miracle of miracles, she finished the last paper before tires scrunched on her drive. Joel had volunteered to stop by to pick up pizzas on his way from town to save her a trip, and the aroma of cheese and sausage followed him into the house when she opened the door to greet him and Adele. She led them into the kitchen at the back of the house and Joel placed the pizzas on the small, round oak table for four.

He looked at his surroundings. "Nice place. I love your AGA."

Miriam snorted. "The AGA and I are incompatible. I always struggle with it." She grinned at Adele. "Hey, nice to meet you."

Adele's gaze drifted to the view of the lake out the kitchen windows. "You live on water and you have pretty flowers."

"Do you like to garden?" Miriam tried to imitate English gardens—planting her beds with delphiniums, roses, and daisies. In the shady spots, she had hostas and daylilies. She could spend hours outside, playing in her flowerbeds.

Adele pressed her lips together, embarrassed. "I just like flowers."

"What's wrong with that?" Miriam asked. "So do I." She put paper plates on the table and went to the refrigerator. "What do you want to drink?"

"Do you have beer?" Joel asked.

"Ah, you need to visit the fridge in the garage." Miriam motioned him to the door off the living room. "I keep the beer in that." She led the way and chose a dark beer for herself. Joel chose an ale, and they returned to Adele in the kitchen. "What about you?" Miriam asked. "What can I get you?"

"Do you have Pepsi?"

"Sure do." Miriam handed her a can and they sat down to eat. Happily, Joel and Adele seemed to be as hungry as she was, and they polished off the pizzas in short order.

"So, how do you like Mill Pond?" Miriam asked Adele.

The girl pursed her lips. Lord, she was pretty, with golden hair and blue eyes. She must look more like her mom. Miriam never would have guessed she had any of Joel's genes. They didn't seem to have anything in common.

Adele sighed. "I miss Grandma and Grandpa," she said, glancing at her dad to see if she'd upset him. "They used to live close to us and they'd take me places, but everyone here is really nice."

Miriam could tell how much Adele worshipped her dad. She didn't want to say anything that would disappoint him. That was sweet. She knew how hard it was for kids who had disabilities to fit in, too. Adele was nineteen but wasn't really an adult. Her mental rating, according to Joel, was twelve years old, but she wasn't a kid. She didn't belong in either world. That made it hard. "You'll meet more and more people," Miriam told her. "And there's lots to do around here."

Adele's gaze went to the water again. "Do you have a boat?"

Miriam nodded. "I have a pontoon and a rowboat, but the pontoon's still at the marina. I don't take it out until school's out and I have more time. Do you want to go sit on the back patio? It's warm enough tonight."

Joel went to get two more beers and Miriam led Adele to the chairs that circled the fire pit outside. When Miriam opened the door, Tommy and Tuppence appeared from their hiding places inside to dash out with them.

"You have cats?" Adele bent to pet Tuppence.

Miriam grabbed Tommy and put him on her lap. "They hide when people they don't know come, but they love being out here. I don't have to worry about them. They never wander far and they come inside when I call them. I trained them when they were kittens."

Adele's blue eyes went wide. "You can train cats? Dad always says they do whatever they want to."

Miriam laughed. "They're pretty independent. That's what I like about them, but I got them from the same litter when they were tiny, and I tied strings to their collars and hooked them to bricks so that when they went too far, the strings yanked them back. Now, they pretty much stay in my yard."

"I love cats." Adele gasped with surprise when Tuppence jumped on her lap and rolled over for her to pet her stomach and chin. "Your cat likes me!"

"My cats like attention. They'll drive you crazy if you don't pet them."

Adele was petting away when Joel stepped out of the cottage and stopped to stare at them. First, he looked surprised, and then he looked sappy. Miriam shook her head at him. "Take a load off and give me my beer."

He blinked and shook his head. Then he came to flop into the lawn chair next to hers. "You have a nice setup."

"Yeah, I like my creature comforts." She took a long swig of her beer, and then Tuppence left Adele to jump on her lap.

Adele looked at the rowboat. "Can we take a ride on the lake?"

Miriam shrugged. "If you wear a life jacket and your dad does all the rowing. This is my lazy day."

Joel huffed a laugh. "I saw the piles of papers you graded today."

"Okay," Miriam amended. "This is my lazy night."

"Good enough." He motioned to Adele. "We won't go far. We'll be back soon."

Miriam watched them push away and follow the shoreline until they reached the reedy patch of water where the channel emptied into the lake. Then they started back. Adele's lips moved the entire time and Joel nodded often, encouraging her. She was obviously excited.

The sun was starting to set when Joel pulled the rowboat back up the bank and propped it against the sycamore tree in Miriam's yard. Miriam pushed to her feet and started toward the kitchen. "Want some tea?"

She fidgeted with the AGA, but it didn't cooperate. "Damn thing!" She gave it a kick before Joel came to help her. The traitorous stove lit on his second try, and soon they had boiled water. Miriam chose Constant Comment tea, but Joel and Adele settled on a hot chocolate mix for their drinks. They sat outside and watched the last hint of pink leave the sky before they went to the living room to get comfortable.

Joel glanced at the books on her built-in bookshelves and looked at her, surprised. "*Dead Men Do Tell Tales? A Handbook for Poisoners?*"

She smirked. "For mysteries. I like to solve the case before the detective does."

Adele picked up the TV's remote and found a show she enjoyed. "Is it okay if I watch this?"

"Go for it. It's Saturday night." Miriam turned on the lamp next to her end of the sofa.

Joel dropped into the armchair opposite her. "This is personal, so if you don't want to answer, just tell me, but have you ever been married?"

Miriam snorted. "No takers."

"Do you come from a big family?"

"Two sisters. Both married. One has kids. We're close."

Joel's lips pinched together. "We used to go to my parents' for meals every Sunday. Adele's going to miss that."

"So come with me to my family's meal tomorrow. We get together twice a month. The more, the merrier."

He grinned. "Easy for you to say. You don't cook."

He had her there. "I bring the wine and beer. With my family, that's a commitment."

He laughed. "Can I bring something?"

"Just you and Adele. We'll make you feel welcome."

His expression softened again. "I can't tell you how nice this was for us tonight. Thank you."

"No biggie." She walked him and Adele to the door when they stood to leave. She watched the car head back toward town and realized she'd enjoyed herself, too. Joel was easy to spend time with. Then she called her mom. "I'm bringing someone for our family meal tomorrow."

"A man?" Her mother sounded too hopeful.

"Not like that. Someone new to Mill Pond," she said and explained.

"Sounds like the man needs a little TLC. He'll like Neil. Your sister's husband loves to yak as much as he loves beer."

When Miriam got ready for bed, she thought about Joel again. He'd face trial by fire tomorrow. Her family was loud and boisterous, people talking on top of one another. They weren't Italian, but you'd never know it. If he survived them, he'd be a shoe-in for Mill Pond.

Daphne called just before she turned the lights off. She and Daphne kept close tabs on each other. They'd been best friends forever. "How did supper go with Joel and Adele?"

"It was nice. He's devoted to his daughter. I don't think I'm getting laid, though. He's all about starting his microbrewery and taking care of Adele, maybe even his brother."

"That's a tall order." Daphne yawned.

"I heard that," Miriam told her. "You waited as long as you could before you called, so you wouldn't interrupt my night. But you're dead on your feet, I can tell. Get some sleep."

"Are you crashing now?"

"I'm already under my blankets. I invited Joel to my family's big meal tomorrow."

"You did?" Daphne sounded more alert.

"Don't read anything into it. The man's lonely and the kid misses her grandparents."

"You're a good person."

"Yeah, but don't put that on my tombstone. How boring. I want something interesting like *Glad This Bitch Is Dead*."

Daphne laughed. "We have to get together soon."

"Let me finish out the school year and then you'll get sick of me."

"I never get sick of you." Another yawn. "But I'm pooped. See you later."

"'Night, friend." And Miriam turned out her light. She rolled over onto her side and her cats nuzzled into their favorite spots. She listened to the water lap on the shore of the lake before sleep claimed her.

# Chapter 7

When Joel pulled onto the asphalt drive that led to Miriam's parents' house, he spotted Miriam's older-model Mercedes parked next to two SUVs near the back door. He turned to Adele. "This must be the place." It wasn't that far from his microbrewery. "Nice house, isn't it?"

The wide, gray bungalow with white trim sat in the center of a large yard surrounded by farmland, but the fields stretched to a barn and silo farther down the road. Joel guessed Miriam's parents only owned the house and the property it sat on. A swing dangled from a huge willow tree in the front yard. A small gray barn served as a garage. A picturesque setting. Two teenage boys were shooting hoops at the backboard attached above the garage door. Joel parked far enough away not to bother them, and they turned and waved when he and Adele started toward the back of the house.

The door opened and a short, plump woman came hurrying toward them. Her dark hair, streaked with gray, was pulled back in a bun. "You must be Joel and Adele!" An apron covered the front of her body. She wore jeans and a long-sleeved T-shirt, and a smile tilted her lips. She went straight to Adele and crushed her in a hug. "You're as pretty as Miriam said you were."

His daughter's face glowed with happiness and Joel's heart swelled with pride. She was a sucker for compliments.

The woman let go of Adele and turned to him. "I'm Penny, Miriam's mom. Come on in and join the fun." A large patio held clusters of lawn furniture and a fire pit. She passed them by and led them into the house.

They entered a large kitchen with an arch that opened into an even bigger dining room. Joel's mouth watered. The aroma of beef, onions, tomatoes, and garlic filled the room. People milled around the long farm table that served as a work island, prepping food, and when Miriam glanced up and saw them, she came over to make introductions. She motioned toward a woman to her left. She was as tall as Miriam, with auburn hair that frizzed to her shoulders.

"This is my sister, Sue-Ellen. She and her husband, Neil, run the florist and honey shop closer to town." She pointed out the window to the two teenage boys, both tall, who were shooting hoops. "Those are her kids."

Joel held out a hand in greeting, but a man with a rangy build and graying hair came up behind him and smacked him on the shoulder.

"I'm Neil, Sue-Ellen's better half. Nice to meet you."

Joel winced from the smack but smiled as he gestured to his daughter. "This is Adele."

Miriam's mother came over to tug her to the other side of the worktable. "Don't get any ideas. She's mine. We need to start dishing up."

Adele beamed, happy to be included, and Neil led Joel to Miriam's other sister, Clair, equally tall, with dark hair pulled back in a ponytail. Joel glanced at a man who was six four with red hair at the end of the table. Neil grinned and nodded. "Yup, the girls all got their dad's height." He hitched a thumb to the man her dad was talking to. "Clair's husband, Max."

If Joel could remember all the names, he'd consider himself lucky. Miriam tried to steal him away, but Neil wasn't ready for that yet. He shoved a beer in Joel's hand and said, "Glad Miriam invited you today. You get to meet the whole family. Heard you moved here to open a microbrewery. Now, that's right up my alley."

"You make beer, too?" Joel asked.

Neil laughed. "Hell no, but I love to drink it. I make honey."

They talked about bees and hives until Miriam's mom clapped her hands and said, "Everyone grab something to carry to the table. It's chow time."

Miriam grabbed a huge Dutch oven filled with mashed potatoes. Neil and Max each carried a platter of Swiss steak. Green beans, sautéed with onions and bacon, followed. The sisters brought bowls of tossed salad, one for each end of the long harvest table and the boys brought baskets of rolls. Penny sat at one end and placed Adele close to her. Her husband sat at the opposite end. Miriam took Joel's hand to seat him next to her. The gesture surprised and pleased him. So did her touch.

Sitting by her side, Joel couldn't help but notice that she sat higher than he did, but that helped him focus on her sharp cheekbones, smooth olive complexion, and pointy chin. She wasn't a soft woman, and he liked that.

When everyone was seated, Penny's husband rose, looked at Joel, and said, "I'm Miriam's dad, Phil. Nice to meet you. Now let's eat."

People dove in and the noise level escalated.

"Hey, pass the butter," one of the boys called.

Sue-Ellen wagged a finger at him. "You can wait till it reaches you, like everyone else."

Max ladled sauce over his mashed potatoes and glanced at Phil. "Did you make it to the golf course this week?"

"Three times. Did some decent putts."

Miriam turned to Joel. "Dad loves golf. Since he retired as a salesman, he can hit the links as many times as he likes."

Her dad's gaze locked with his. "Do you play golf, Joel?"

"Sorry, I never took it up."

"Just as well; it's addictive. Clair plays, and so does Max, but they make me work too hard. Our Clair's always been good at sports; why she went into teaching phys ed."

Joel looked at Clair. "What grades do you teach?"

"Elementary." She pushed a strand of hair that had escaped her ponytail behind her ear. She struck him as shyer than the rest. "Max teaches middle-school science."

Joel chuckled. "Between the three of you, you have every school building in town covered."

Miriam cleaned her plate and motioned for more mashed potatoes. The woman could eat! "You've got that right. We like to keep the kids in Mill Pond on their toes."

Her family obviously took kids seriously. At the other end of the table, her mom and Sue-Ellen were asking Adele all kinds of questions about her favorite movies and music, keeping her involved in the conversation. This wasn't a children-should-be-seen-and-not-heard family. The kids were an integral part of it.

When everyone was finished eating, the men rose to clear the table and the women went to the kitchen to carry in dessert. Joel stared at the two pineapple upside-down cakes and decided he'd hit the jackpot today. Miriam's family cooked like his mom used to. Since he and his brother, Miles, had grown up and moved out of the house, Mom only bothered with big meals on Sundays, but he sure loved it when she invited them for supper.

As always, when he thought about Miles, he worried. Joel knew Miles hadn't quit drinking, but he was managing somehow, showing up for work every day. Somehow, he was coping. If that changed, though, it would be better if he could move him here and keep an eye on him.

When Phil finished the last bite of his second piece of cake, people streamed to the kitchen, and each one seemed to have a job. Sue-Ellen's boys rinsed the dishes, Miriam and Clair each loaded a dishwasher. Joel was surprised to see there were two of them. Neil parceled leftovers into Baggies for people to take home and Joel and Adele were assigned the job of wiping down the dining room table. The pace was fast and efficient, and then the boys took off to go outside. Everyone else started out after them.

Joel looked puzzled. "Where are we going?"

Phil answered. "The boys have challenged us to a game of PIG. We always do something after we eat."

Penny walked to the fire pit in the backyard and motioned for Adele to join her to watch. Everyone else lined up to shoot hoops.

The boys started with a three-point shot, and Phil, Sue-Ellen, and Neil all missed to earn a *P*. Five shots later, Sue-Ellen, Neil, and their grandpa had been eliminated from the game, Max had *P-I*, and Joel had a *P*. When they were kids, Joel and Miles had played HORSE every chance they got. They were both too short to make their high school team, but they got really good at hitting the basket. Joel watched as Miriam sank another shot. He raised an eyebrow at her.

"I was on the girls' team all through high school," she told him. "I'm going to crush you."

She wouldn't win any awards for femininity, but he had to give her an A+ for confidence. He grinned up at her. "In your dreams."

Her eyes went wide, then she threw back her head and laughed. "Good luck, little man."

Oh, she was going to eat her words. He intended to beat her if it took everything he had.

Then the boys, who'd controlled the game so far, got in a hurry and missed a hard shot. Clair was next up to shoot, and that's when the game changed. Miriam's sister didn't miss. Ever. Miriam went out next.

As she left the court, Joel held out a hand and said, "Sorry to see you go. Okay, not that sorry. Remember, I'm still in the game. You're not."

A smirk curled her lips. "Maybe I underestimated you."

He wiggled his eyebrows at her. "That always works to my advantage."

She narrowed her eyes, studying him more closely. "Are you any good at Wiffle ball?"

"Miles and I were in Little League for years."

She grimaced. "Golf?"

"No."

"Then we'll putt the next time you come."

That surprised him. "Is it that important to you to win?"

She shrugged her shoulders. "Don't give a fig one way or the other. I just don't want you to get a big head."

He laughed as Clair sank another shot. Max went out next. Finally, Clair hit a tricky side shot Joel and both boys couldn't make. She won the game. Joel went to slump in a chair close to Adele and Miriam reached over to pat him on the head.

"You've learned your place in the world, friend. Women rule."

He'd never argue with that. To him, women set the tone of a house. He'd build a pedestal for his mother if she'd sit down and rest on it. "Great, I'll make you my queen."

Miriam laughed again. She thought he was joking.

He wasn't. He loved how strong the women in this family were. They owned their power. When he looked up, he saw Miriam's mom watching him. She had a gleam in her eye. That gave him confidence. He got the feeling Penny was rooting for him. He also had the feeling it would take every trick he knew to catch her daughter.

Once Clair had been announced victor, everyone meandered back into the house and headed to the living room to visit. People talked about their week, any new news, and anything they'd heard of interest. Joel thought he'd feel like an outsider, but he enjoyed their camaraderie. So did Adele. Finally, when the clock hit four, people started to leave. Joel took that as his cue and rose, too.

"Thanks for inviting us. We really enjoyed ourselves." Miriam's parents were the best. "You made us feel like part of Mill Pond."

"You *are* part of the town now." Phil patted his shoulder; must be a family trait. "Miriam will have to bring you again some time."

"We'd like that."

On the drive home, Adele never quit talking. It had been a long time since he'd seen her so animated. He'd have to make a point of doing something fun with her every Sunday. They were making a great start in Mill Pond. He wanted to keep it going that way.

# Chapter 8

Miriam poised with her pen over her paper. "Okay, Mark, who are you going to interview?"

"Coach Stafford. Without him, I wouldn't have a football scholarship to IU."

Miriam nodded. Mark hurried out of the room and she turned to Alicia. "You?"

"Principal Snyder. He knows every kid in this building. He's special."

He sure as hell was. He always put his students first. Miriam nodded, and Alicia took off to start on her assignment. The last person who stood before her was Maya. This would be this year's final edition of the school newspaper, a *Goodbye, Mill Pond High* tribute. Miriam finished every journalism class this way.

Instead of sending Maya on her way, Miriam asked, "So, have you been accepted into any colleges yet?" She had a horrible feeling she had, but that she wasn't acting on it.

Maya bit her bottom lip and looked away.

Miriam sighed. She'd never been good at tiptoeing around issues. "Look, I've seen you with T. J. You're making choices here; you know that, right? Guys can interfere with goals. When I started college, I told myself I'd finish, that nothing would get in my way, not even a boyfriend, that everything else could wait."

Maya shifted her weight from one foot to the other. "I don't know what I want right now. I don't want to leave T. J. I want to stay in Mill Pond."

A scream built inside her, but Miriam stifled it. "You could see T. J. every weekend if you drove home. Mill Pond is close enough to the IU campus."

Maya scrunched her face in a grimace. "We see each other every day. T. J. would find someone else if I left him."

That pissed her off. "Then how much does he care about you? If he can't support your dreams, he doesn't love you."

Maya took a deep breath. "But he does. He just doesn't care about college. And he doesn't like being alone. He's happy here."

Miriam gave her a long, hard look. "But you've always wanted more. You wanted to leave here, to expand your horizons. Are you willing to give everything up for a boy?"

Maya looked uncomfortable. "You made a choice, didn't you? You gave up something. You chose a career over a man and now you're alone."

Ouch! There *had* been a guy who was two years ahead of her in college. When he'd graduated, he wanted her to leave school and move to Texas with him, where he was going to start a job. She'd turned him down. And she'd never regretted it. But she *was* alone now. Would Maya be all right with that? Miriam took a minute to respond. "I had offers, but I never wanted to settle for less. None of the men were a good fit for me and I really wanted to be a teacher."

Maya jutted out her chin. "T. J. *is* right for me. He makes me happy."

"You're eighteen. A lot of things change between now and your early twenties. *You'll* change after you graduate. What makes you happy now might make you miserable in a few years."

Maya crossed her arms over her small chest. "Look at me. I'm never going to be the most attractive girl in the room. Most guys don't even look my way."

"So what?" Miriam knew that feeling. "I'd rather be happy alone than unhappy with someone I don't want to be with. Look, is T. J. the first boy who's ever paid attention to you?"

"What difference does that make?"

"I'm just saying I get it. It's nice to have someone notice you. Every girl's ego can use a few strokes. Hell, mine could. It feels good, but that doesn't mean T. J.'s the one."

"You're wrong. He is."

How did you argue with that? Miriam tried to choose her words carefully. "First, I think you're going to be one of those girls who blossoms into herself. You're going to be surprised how pretty you get in the next year or two. I've seen it happen. But I understand what you're telling me and I'm going to be blunt. There were guys who looked at me and thought I'd be so desperate for attention, I'd be an easy mark. T. J. has gone through his share of girls. Does he just want to have sex with you? Because that won't last."

A fiery blush lit Maya's face. "T. J.'s not like that."

"He's a guy."

"We like to talk to each other. He likes *me*."

"And what happens if you pass on college and three months later you break up? What then? You've given up a full scholarship for nothing."

Maya's expression took on a stubborn look. "I'll worry about that if it happens."

Miriam was getting nowhere fast. She knew when to admit defeat. Sighing, she looked down at her list. "Okay, I just wanted you to think things through. I've said what I wanted to say, so let's get back to classwork. Who do you want to interview today?"

Maya fidgeted with her notebook. "You."

"Me?" Miriam looked up, surprised.

"Everyone knows you're one of the best teachers around. You give it your all. I want to interview you."

It was a wonderful compliment. Miriam would have basked in happiness if she didn't want to throttle Maya more, but she forced a smile. She'd done her best to convince Maya to take the scholarship and failed. She wouldn't use the interview to badger the point into the ground. She gave a quick nod. "Okay, let's do this. Ask away."

Maya started with the question everyone asked. "What made you want to be a teacher?"

"So I could have my summers off." It was a smart-ass answer, and Miriam laughed at Maya's shocked expression. "Not really. I loved school, loved learning. I don't have the patience to teach elementary students, like my sister, so I chose high school. And I've always loved books and English."

The questions got better from there. "Why not become a professor? That has more status, doesn't it?"

Miriam shrugged. "Maybe. I've never worried about status that much. The thing is, I really like kids. I wanted to make a difference in their lives."

"Do you think girls are smarter than boys?"

Miriam laughed. This was the Maya she enjoyed, the girl who

was so original. "Not really. I think we balance out pretty well." Instead of thinking about her students, she thought about Joel. He struck her as having more common sense than scholastic ability. The man was plenty smart, but she'd bet money that if she saw one of his old report cards, he didn't excel at school. There were all kinds of smarts. And all of them mattered.

After a few more questions, Maya ended the interview by asking, "If you could do anything differently, what would it be?"

"Phew! A tough one." Miriam thought a minute. An answer whispered in her mind, but she pushed it aside. *I'd find me a man* didn't sound like an appropriate response for the school newspaper and it certainly wouldn't help Maya. "I'd travel more," she said. "See more of the world."

"By yourself?" Maya bit her bottom lip the minute the words popped out.

Miriam grinned, feeling daring. "Why not? I don't mind going to movies alone and I eat in restaurants solo. What's wrong with traveling single?"

Maya stared for a minute. "Doesn't it get lonely?"

"With my friends and family?" Miriam leaned closer to make her point. "I can always call someone or stop by for a visit. Some people feel alone in a crowd. I'm not one of them. I tend to start yakking to someone, and pretty soon, I'm connected. I like people."

"And you're that sure that they'll like you back?"

Miriam blinked. She'd never doubted someone would enjoy her company. "I'm not going to win them all," she admitted. "And that's okay. Who wants to be around someone they don't click with? And I might not make friends for life with a bunch of strangers, but it's all about finding something in common. Most people are more alike than different."

Maya's voice dipped and she sounded unsure of herself. "You're lucky. You like yourself."

Miriam reached out to touch Maya's hand. "You should like yourself, too. You're pretty wonderful; you just don't realize it."

Maya gave a quick nod, blinking rapidly, and looked at her notes. She forced a smile. "Well, thank you for the interview. I'll write it up and turn it in tomorrow."

The bell to change classes rang. Miriam watched Maya hurry out of the room. Now she understood the girl more. Maya needed to feel loved, accepted. T. J. did that for her now. Her mother had rejected her. She felt awkward, unattractive, and socially inept. A lot of high school nerds did. Miriam got that. But the girl was taking a huge risk. She wanted someone to be there for her, and T. J. made it sound like he would be. Miriam hoped it would last, but they were just kids. The odds were against them.

# Chapter 9

On Monday night, Tyne and Daphne invited Miriam, Joel, and Adele to their log cabin for supper. Adele squirmed on the front seat as they turned in the opposite direction from the lake to leave town and head toward the national forest.

"Friends have invited us out two days in a row!" She pointed as they passed Mill Pond High. "That's where Miriam teaches, isn't it?"

"Yup. She'll be at Tyne and Daphne's, too."

"I like her."

"So do I." They turned and watched farm fields blend from one to the next on both sides of the road. Adele oohed when cows leaned over a fence close to the road to eat tall grass near the berm. "I could touch them."

"They're happy eating their special treats. Let's let them enjoy themselves."

She held her nose when they passed a pig farm.

"Stinks, doesn't it?" Joel was glad he wasn't a close neighbor. He wondered if you ever got used to the smell if you lived with it day in and day out.

Adele smiled and nodded, then pointed at the view ahead. "Look at all the trees!"

"That's the national forest. We'll have to take a ride and stop to picnic there in the fall, when the leaves change. I've heard it's beautiful."

When he pulled into the drive for Tyne and Daphne's log cabin, Adele stared. "It looks like *Little House in the Big Woods*." She was a Laura Ingalls Wilder fan. Joel had read her every book in the series and then he'd bought the DVDs of the TV show based on them. "Can we have a log cabin, Dad? One with a green tin roof like this?"

Joel chuckled. "I don't know if there are any for sale. We'll have to see what's on the market."

She opened her door, anxious to step onto the long front porch and sit in one of the rockers. Then she noticed Miriam's car parked near the garage. "Miriam's here! Come on, Dad. Hurry!"

Usually, he was waiting on his daughter. This was a fun flip. "I'm on my way." He placed his hand under her elbow to help her up the steps. She could manage them herself, but it always made him nervous.

"Will Tyne be here?" His daughter had been quite taken by him.

"Tyne and his wife. You like Daphne. She's always nice to you when she checks on you when I'm away."

"Daphne." Joel watched the pieces of the puzzle fall into place for her. "Daphne's Tyne's wife."

"Right."

Adele smiled. "A prince and a princess." Like the Disney movies she watched over and over again—two beautiful people who were perfect together.

"Exactly." Joel knocked on the door and it flew open seconds later.

"Hey, glad you made it!" Tyne motioned them inside.

Tyne had Monday nights off and loved to cook for his wife and her friends. That boggled Joel's mind. After all, the man did breakfast and lunch shifts on Sundays and Mondays and the night shifts on Tuesdays through Saturdays. If Joel cooked seven days a week like Tyne did, he'd opt for takeout on his night off.

"I don't cook every Monday," Tyne told him when Joel asked about it. He led Joel and Adele into the cabin's large, open great room. "But we like to entertain and it's impossible during the week."

Daphne, Joel knew, went to eat supper with her parents on Tuesdays and Fridays, and she met Miriam at Chase's bar on Thursdays. Most Wednesdays, she drove to Ian's inn to eat in the kitchen with her husband. She usually stayed in her stained-glass shop in town until then, and Joel would give her a wave when he zipped up to his apartment.

Tyne motioned Adele to the sitting area to join Daphne and Miriam. "Make yourself at home. The girls have been waiting on you."

Adele hovered a little, uncertain, and Joel took a minute to look around. He gave a nod of approval. Open areas were the rage now. Wheat-colored walls and hardwood floors made the space warm and inviting. Two rocking chairs were pulled to the fireplace at the back of the room and Miriam occupied one of them.

She waved at Adele. "Hey, kid, come keep me company."

Adele ditched him in a heartbeat and Tyne chuckled. "Come on. I'll show you our gardens in the backyard. I kept supper simple tonight for Miriam. She's a meat and potatoes girl, so I cooked porchetta and cheesy scalloped potatoes."

*Simple*. Right. Simple, for Joel, meant a ham sandwich.

They walked out the kitchen door into a decent-size yard, surrounded by a white picket fence. "Shadow stays inside the fence so we don't have to worry about him."

Joel frowned. "Shadow?"

"Our cat." Tyne grinned. "He disappears when strangers come, but he'll grow braver when the food's on the table." He led Joel to a row of raised beds. "I weeded everything today."

The rows of spinach, lettuces, and herbs were in perfect order. Joel got the idea that for such a low-key demeanor, Tyne was a bit of a perfectionist. He looked up to gaze at the view on the other side of the fence. The national forest stretched into the distance. "Wow. This is nice."

Tyne nodded. "There's a trail that runs right behind our house." He nodded for Joel to follow him back inside. "The girls will be getting hungry. They're friendlier if you feed them."

Adele got cranky when she was hungry, too. That was why Joel tried to keep the refrigerator and cupboards stocked with healthy snacks. She'd forget about eating when she was watching TV, but the minute a show ended, she went in search of sustenance.

Daphne came to help Tyne carry things to the table. Tyne arranged the pork roast surrounded with carrots, parsnips, and onions onto a brightly painted platter.

"From Mexico," Tyne said. An elaborately painted dish held Brussels sprouts with bacon. "From Thailand." And then there was the heavy casserole with scalloped potatoes. "Stoneware," Tyne said, "from an Indian reservation in Arizona."

"How much have you traveled?" Joel knew Tyne had moved from place to place as a chef, but the guy must have gotten around.

"Europe, Mexico, South America, Thailand." Tyne sat down across from his wife. Joel took the spot across from Miriam and Adele. "I'll tell you about it someday."

Joel would love to hear about the places Tyne had been. He'd always wanted to travel, but he'd married right out of high school and April and Adele had dictated his life from that moment on.

"Dig in." Tyne sipped a beer as everyone loaded their plates.

Miriam went straight for the porchetta. "*Mmm.*" She leaned back in her chair and closed her eyes. "I've never tasted a roast this good."

Neither had Joel. "You must have rubbed it with special seasonings. It's delicious."

"Anything for you, E.T.," Tyne teased her.

Miriam grinned at his nickname for her.

Adele licked her lips. "Can you buy this someplace special?"

"Not the way I make it. I'm a chef." Tyne shrugged. "Roasts are easy. I injected this one with a special blend I made, then rubbed it with spices. All simple steps."

At Adele's blank look, he pared it down for her. "You sprinkle it with herbs and salt, then you let it dry in the refrigerator for a while and throw it in the oven."

Adele caught most of that and Miriam beamed her approval at Tyne. Joel's heart clutched, and he realized he wanted Miriam to look at him like that. Silly. He didn't know her that well, but she sure intrigued him.

Miriam's smile widened. "The pork's great, but I'm stealing some leftover potatoes. They're to die for."

Daphne pointed to a large plastic container on the countertop. "For you. I told Tyne you'd want them. I thought you'd need something cheesy and gooey to make you feel better about Maya."

Miriam's lips pinched into a tight line and Joel frowned. Talk about an abrupt mood change. "What's up with Maya?"

Miriam's words were clipped. "She's giving up a scholarship to stay here with T. J."

Tyne sliced more roast for second helpings and put some on Miriam's plate. "Paula wasn't happy when Steph passed on culinary school to stay in Mill Pond with Ben, but that's worked out great."

Miriam pushed away her plate and snorted. "You and Paula still trained her. How could that not go well?"

"I'm just saying, Maya's a smart girl. She'll figure out something."

Miriam didn't look convinced, so Daphne tried a different kind of distraction. "Have you heard the news? Guess who has to get married?"

Miriam's blue eyes glittered with curiosity. "Spit it out. What's the scoop?"

Daphne sounded smug when she said, "Chantelle."

Miriam's jaw dropped. She glanced Tyne's way. "The hussy who always tries to feel you up?"

"One and the same." Tyne quirked an eyebrow. "Once I married Daphne, everyone else got the message. Not her."

Miriam finished her potatoes and licked the sauce off her fork. "Who's the unlucky man?"

"Eddie Jork. They weren't careful enough." Daphne sounded almost sorry for him.

Miriam licked her lips and gazed at the refrigerator. "Is there dessert?"

"When isn't there?" Tyne stood to clear the table. Joel rose to help him.

Daphne went on with her gossip. "People are saying that Eddie's thrilled about the wedding."

"He probably thinks he's scored a prize." When Tyne opened the refrigerator, Miriam leaned forward to see what was inside. She gasped when he carried a trifle to the table.

Adele's eyes went round. "Do we eat that?"

Joel patted her shoulder. "It's almost too pretty to touch, isn't it?"

"But wait till you taste it." Daphne gave a devilish grin. "It's so good, you can't help yourself. Tyne makes the whipping cream from scratch."

Adele had no idea what that meant. As far as she knew, whipped cream only came in a can. When Tyne scooped a helping into a fancy glass and handed it to her, she stared at it in awe.

Joel picked up a spoon and dipped it into the dessert, then held it out for his daughter. She took a bite and moaned.

Miriam laughed. "That's what Tyne's cooking does to me, too."

"That's what Chantelle must do for poor Eddie." When Tyne looked at Daphne, surprised, she put a hand over her lips, but her eyes sparkled too much for her to be contrite.

"How you've changed." And Tyne sounded like he thoroughly enjoyed it.

Joel was surprised by how catty the girls could be but decided he liked it. They didn't pretend and their comments cracked him up.

They were halfway through their trifle when Shadow came to rub against Daphne's ankles. When she bent to pet him, he meowed.

"You have a cat!" For Adele, Tyne and Daphne's house had just about everything a person could want.

"He wants me to feed him." When Daphne didn't move right away, the cat stalked to the kitchen and jumped on the sink top, next to the roast.

"Oh no you don't!" Tyne hurried out to rescue the meat. He picked up the cat's bowl and shredded some of the pork into it, then covered the rest.

The cat finished his supper, then jumped on the counter to lick whipping cream out of the mixing bowl. Daphne went to save that, putting it in the sink to soak, then gave Shadow a small sample.

Adele giggled. "Your cat's spoiled."

"You'd think a stray would have better manners, wouldn't you? That he'd appreciate a good home?" But when the cat finished eating, Daphne scooped him up and held him close. Purrs filled the room. When he wanted down, she gave him one last stroke before he stretched on the floor beside her and lifted his paw to lick it.

Miriam turned to Adele. "Have you had any pets? You liked my cats, too."

Adele shook her head and glanced at Joel. "Grandma and Grandpa have a dog, Farley, but I only get to visit him. Mom didn't like animals, said they were too much work. And when we moved away from her, Dad said he was too busy to take care of pets."

Miriam sent him a sympathetic look. "Your dad's right. Pets are a lot of work, but if you ever want to visit Tommy and Tuppence, they'd love to see you."

"Really?" Adele sounded excited.

"Once school's out at the end of the month, you'll have to come spend a day with me. Your dad can work and we can hang out together, but I have too much going on right now."

Adele nodded. "Dad says we're going to be here a long time. We won't move before school's out."

Her answer surprised Miriam, Joel could tell. "Good! That way you and I have a date."

They all helped with cleanup after dessert, and then Joel and Adele took their leave. "Thanks for a great supper. This is your night off, though, so we'll leave you to enjoy the rest of it."

Miriam left, too, carrying a hefty supply of scalloped potatoes with her. Before she climbed in her old Mercedes, she turned to Joel. "If I were a nice person, I'd offer to share this with you, but it's not gonna happen."

"We have plenty of groceries at home," he assured her. "No worries."

They drove off in opposite directions and Joel sighed.

Adele stared at him. "Did you want some of the potatoes?"

"No, hon. I'm just happy we had such a nice night." He always enjoyed himself when he was around Miriam.

Adele smiled. "Me too. I like it here."

So did he. Mill Pond had lots more potential than he'd ever dreamed of.

# Chapter 10

Joel asked Adele one last time, "Are you sure you don't want to come with me?"

Plopped on the couch in front of the TV, she shook her head, ignoring him. She could be stubborn when she wanted to be. She'd had more people time than usual, and now she wanted to retreat into her own private world.

She'd better enjoy it while she could. Once they got drywall up in the brewery, he was going to make her a little space of her own in his office with a cozy chair and a TV. That way, she could go with him at work. He could keep an eye on her.

He motioned toward an insulated lunch box on the coffee table. "I packed you a sandwich and snacks. Remember to eat something."

She didn't hear him. She was already lost in TV land. He went to stand in front of her to block the screen. He pointed to the lunch box in front of her. "Eat this when your cell phone alarm goes off or I'm not letting you stay home the next time I go to work."

That got her attention. "Promise," she told him. She wouldn't remember on her own, but she would when the alarm went off.

He gave her a quick peck on the cheek and headed out the door. Daphne had said she'd check on her a few times during the day. When he reached the bottom of the stairs, he glanced in her shop. Lots of customers. Business in Mill Pond was picking up the warmer the days got. He wanted to open the brewery in July, if everything went well. Tourists would clog the town by then.

When Joel reached the dairy, Nick Hillegard's silver pickup was already parked near the back door. Nick lived in Mill Pond and had plenty of building experience. He'd worked with his dad since he could hold a wrench. He was a contractor and a plumber and flipped houses on the side. His older brother, Brian, was an electrician, and Joel had hired him, too, to help convert the place into a microbrewery and hot dog joint.

Nick followed Joel inside and whistled when he studied the large space. "You're going to work with us, right? Because this is a big project."

Joel nodded. "I used to buy strip malls and fix them up. I'm handy enough with a hammer and drywall."

"I've heard that before." Nick glanced at the blueprints Joel cradled under one arm. "What have you got in mind?"

Joel spread them out on a card table he'd brought earlier. He'd already given Nick a rough idea of the building's measurements and his plans. "I want a family room at the back of the building, and I'll separate it from the bar with the brewery and bottling room, then a small office over here and the kitchen opposite them. I'm going to pour a cement patio by the side door." He pointed as he spoke. "I'd like the brewery to have two huge inside windows so people can see the process."

Nick nodded. "I like it. Easy enough to do. What are you going to do about the ceiling?"

Beams spanned the space high above their heads.

"I want to leave them open, give the place an industrial feel. We might have to insulate the roof and walls, though, and install massive ceiling fans." Joel pointed to where the brewery room would be. "We'll need lots of pipes and plumbing." He planned on using steam heat to brew the beer.

Nick studied the sturdy structure for more details. "There are already plenty of pipes in here. We should be able to come up with something."

That's what Joel had thought, too.

"What are you going to serve to drink in the family room?" Nick studied the blueprint. Joel's office would hide the brewery from sight, so that kids couldn't see the beer.

"Root beer, sodas, the usual. I want to make my own root beer." There was a door to the brewery so that waitresses could easily access the room.

"And what do you need in the kitchen? Special equipment?"

Joel handed him a layout of the future kitchen. "I have everything ordered. They can deliver whenever we're ready."

Nick gave another whistle. "I think you're right. We can start work today, and if nothing unexpected happens, this is a pretty straightforward job."

"What about building supplies?"

Nick looked at his watch. "I ordered enough framing and drywall to get started and my crew will be here in ten minutes."

Even better than Joel had expected. "I love working with good people."

"And we love working for people who pay cash. That's the one thing about taking on small jobs. You can end up chasing the money."

Joel knew about that from his days of renting out small business spaces, but Nick looked too young to have that kind of experience. "How old are you?" he asked.

Nick grinned. "Older than I look. I'm twenty-eight, but my boyish charm makes everyone guess younger."

"Is that what it is?" The kid was attractive enough, with brown, wavy hair, dark eyes, and deep dimples. His nose was crooked, and Joel guessed he'd broken it. "You flip houses around here, right?"

"Nope, I mostly buy and sell in Indy. A great place to meet women."

That caught Joel by surprise. "Is that why you work there?"

"Not really, it's a bigger market, easier to move houses, but hot girls are an added benefit."

"Because it's a bigger market?" Joel teased.

"Lots more bars, more nightlife."

Nick didn't strike Joel as a partier. He seemed like a hometown boy, the type who'd put down roots and stay in Mill Pond. "You didn't find a girl you liked here?"

Nick's gaze slid away from his. "One, but she's not interested, so I spread my net wider. I met Roxy at a concert four months ago."

"She must have struck a chord."

"She's a city girl, all in to going out and having fun. She's on the expensive side, but she's always a good time."

Joel frowned. "A party girl?"

"I guess you could call her that."

Joel had a bad feeling. He'd met girls like that after he'd divorced April. Met them, period. Once he mentioned he had a daughter, they disappeared. Miles had blown through a few of them, though. The girls had stuck around until his money ran out, then they were history. "Do you two have anything in common?"

Nick shrugged. "We both like to drink and have fun."

It was none of his business, he knew, but he still asked, "And that's enough for you for now?"

Nick raised a dark eyebrow. "You're divorced, right?"

Joel liked Nick more already. The guy didn't pull his punches. "Yeah, and you learn from your mistakes. Mine: Don't try to rescue a woman in distress."

"Jodie's not like that."

"No, she's the let's-enjoy-the-moment type. And when you get stale, she'll move on."

"And you know that because . . ."

"My brother fell for her type."

Nick stopped to study him. "So what do you recommend, now that you're older and wiser?"

"Damned if I know. I only know what *doesn't* work. This time, though, I'm looking for a woman who doesn't need me, who can cope without a man. Then, if she chooses me, it's because I'll add something to her life and she wants me around."

Nick was silent a moment. "You've had some tough times, haven't you?"

"You don't want to know. But you live and you learn. Either that or you repeat your mistakes. That, I don't want to do."

Nick was about to say more when the sound of a big truck pulling close to the building cut him off. "Our supplies are here. Our crew will be close behind."

*Thank heavens!* Joel had surprised himself by turning into a love guru, dispensing unwanted advice to his poor contractor. Where the hell had that come from? He usually tried his best to stay out of other peoples' business. Maybe Mill Pond, and the way everyone knew everyone else, was having a strange effect on him. He took a deep breath and walked out to meet the suppliers.

Nick's three-man crew came five minutes later, and Joel took one look at them and ordered pizzas to be delivered for lunch at noon. These men looked serious. They were ready to dig in and get things done. If he fed them, they'd get a lot done today.

They started with framing out rooms. The sound of nail guns and heavy equipment echoed off the cement block walls and cement floors. Those cement walls got a moisture barrier installed over them before insulation. The floors would be sealed and painted.

When Joel left the building at five that night, he was sweaty and filthy. He, Nick, and the three men had stopped for a quick lunch, then worked the rest of the day. Joel couldn't wait to get home and take a shower.

Daphne's yellow SUV was already gone when he parked behind the stained-glass shop. He let himself in with his key and climbed the back stairs to his apartment. The aroma of burned beef hit him the minute he opened the door. Adele was fixated on a Disney movie and didn't look up when he hurried to the kitchen and turned off the slow cooker. He wrinkled his nose when he lifted the lid. She'd put in a beef roast, nothing more. No broth. No water.

He took a deep breath to try to collect himself. This wouldn't have started a fire. The worst that could have happened was that he'd have to throw away the slow cooker and the meat. Adele would be safe.

He unplugged the cord and went to sit beside his daughter. "The beef's dead. It looks like a hockey puck."

She turned to him, surprised. "What?"

"It looks like you tried to make a roast. You didn't add any liquid. It's dead."

Her face crumpled.

"No big deal. I'm going to toss the whole thing out." Then she wouldn't be tempted to use the slow cooker again. "What would you like for supper?"

Her eyes lit up. She was so easily distracted. "Can we get burgers?"

"I've heard that Ralph's Diner makes burgers to die for. Want to go there tonight?"

"We're going out again?"

"Why not? This is a fresh start. We'll meet more people."

Adele glanced at her TV, torn.

"You finish your show and I'll take a shower. How's that? No hurry. And then we'll go to Ralph's."

She nodded, happy again. She turned and pushed Play on the TV. Once the show started, she was lost to him.

# Chapter 11

Over the next two weeks Joel settled into a routine. He bought a recliner and had it delivered to the brewery so he could take Adele with him to work every morning. Each day he packed her laptop, along with DVDs of her favorite movies, and she watched them while he and the crew worked. They moved her from spot to spot to avoid sawdust. As long as she had her shows to watch, she didn't mind.

At lunch time they all drove to Ralph's Diner and he picked up the tab. It was an added expense, but Nick introduced them to everyone in the restaurant and Adele felt like she was a part of things. They broke their routine on Wednesdays, when they went to Chase's bar for BBQ and ate outside on the patio because Adele wasn't twenty-one. After lunch Joel drove her back to their apartment before returning to work. By then, she was ready to cocoon.

One day, Grams and Miguel came to sit at their table and chat. Both of them were serious about gardening. Miguel gave Joel lots of advice about how to landscape the brewery: which plants were no fuss and which were high maintenance. Grams hit up Adele about setting tables to get ready for church suppers, which thrilled his daughter. She loved feeling needed.

Another day, Nick introduced them to David and Darinda Danza.

"We make great chicken sausages," David told him, "if you want something on your menu to appeal to the health-conscious crowd."

"How many kinds of sausages do you make?"

David shook his head. "Friend, if you want a specialty sausage, I can make it for you. We Italians can add garlic, fennel, whatever seasonings you want. Carl Gruber, who raises grass-fed cows, and Cutter Rethlake, who owns a hog farm way out on County Road, and I work together to come up with different blends. Art stocks three of them at his grocery, but we can make a unique one for you."

"I'm in," Joel said. "I need something that will go great with ales, mustard, and sauerkraut."

Not only did they strike a deal but Joel made two new friends.

Ralph and his wife, Jules, who still waitressed at the diner after marrying him, stopped to chat whenever they could. All in all, Joel and Adele were beginning to feel at home here.

Joel made a point of being home at six every night to eat supper with his daughter. He usually made something fast and simple—cheese toasties, pork chops, tacos—but every Tuesday they went to Mill Pond's pizza parlor and met more new people. Garth Roarke, who ran the garage at the edge of town, ate there each Tuesday with his wife, Leona.

Tonight, when Joel and Adele walked in to eat, Leona looked up and waved them to their table. A hairdresser, she looked at Adele's thick, wavy blond hair and shook her head. "You just washed it, didn't you? Bet you don't have to do anything special to make it look pretty. Look at your waves."

Adele turned a bright shade of pink. Compliments were few and far between, and she repeated them over and over again, something to cherish. Joel turned to listen to Adele's answer as the door opened and Miriam stepped in. Then his focus shifted. She looked tired. Her dark curls drooped as low as her shoulders. She saw him and came to say hello.

Joel glanced at the clock. Six thirty, and Miriam was dressed in khaki pants and a button-down shirt. "Did you just come from school?"

Leona tsk-tsked. "Girl, your hair looks like an overgrown poodle's. It needs a good cut."

"I know, I know. It's the end of the year. Hell month. I stayed late to grade tests so I didn't have to haul them home. My stack's already tall enough." She motioned toward the counter. "I stopped to pick up supper."

She looked like she could crawl in bed and sleep for a month. If this was a teacher's life, Joel would change jobs. "How much longer before you're done?"

"Two weeks, but seniors finish next Friday and my load will get lighter. Memorial Day makes a four-day week after that. Then I'm done."

It was a good thing. It looked like it would take the entire summer for her to recuperate. "You earn your keep, that's for sure."

She laughed. "Glad you noticed. Teachers get no glory." Her pizza came out of the oven and she went to pay for it. "See you when things settle down."

They watched out the window as she drove away. Once she was out of sight, Leona huffed a sigh. "That woman never puts herself first. She could use a spa day—hair, manicure, and facial. She's a mess."

Garth shrugged. "She's never worried about her looks. I think she's owned that blouse since she graduated from college."

Leona gasped. "But she makes good money."

"It's just not something she cares about." Garth looked at his wife's tight yellow pants and high heels. "She's not stylish, like you."

"I think she looks great." Joel hadn't meant to say the words, but they slipped out.

Leona's red lips curled in a smile. "Do you have a thing for E.T.?"

Tyne's nickname for Miriam had obviously spread. "You have to admire her, don't you? She always pushes for the best."

"Not when it comes to fashion." But Leona looked pleased with herself. That was when Joel remembered that someone had told him Leona spread gossip through Mill Pond faster than a brushfire. Oh, well, he *did* think Miriam looked great. So what?

Adele finished her pizza and Garth and Leona stood to leave.

Garth held out a hand to Joel. "Hope you come to one of Grams's church socials sometime. Tessa always brings mighty fine pies."

"Sounds like enough temptation to me." Joel smiled at Adele. "She loves desserts."

On the short drive home Joel thought about the brewery again. In two weeks it would be glassed in and the brew tanks installed. He'd already ordered enough supplies to start his first batch. He intended to produce up to 310 gallons at a time. His brands took three weeks to process. It would take longer than that to finish the building, but if worse came to worse, he could sell beer before he opened the restaurant.

He pulled behind Daphne's shop and opened the pickup's door for Adele. On the way upstairs to their apartment, he grinned. Once he had his first batch of beer done, he could invite Miriam to the brewery for a free trial. School would be out by then. Maybe he could spend more time with her.

# Chapter 12

Miriam watched the clock tick to the final minutes of school on Friday. Thank God. While her students worked on their term papers, she'd graded as many papers as she could, but she kept getting interrupted.

"Miss Reinhardt, am I doing footnotes right?" Corey asked.

"Not yet." Corey needed everything explained to him at least a half dozen times, but once he got it, he kept it forever, so she showed him—again—the correct way to do them.

Marissa was next at her desk. "Miss Reinhardt, are you grading mostly on content? How much of a percentage does grammar count on our grade?"

Miriam had taught diagramming sentences so many times her students should know where to put every comma, but Marissa tended to be a bit on the lazy, impatient side. If she didn't have to worry about it, she wouldn't. "Twenty-five percent." Miriam raised the schoolteacher eyebrow. "You'd better proofread and catch everything you can."

The girl looked disappointed but returned to her seat.

Kids came with question after question until the final period ended and school was out.

Then Miriam sat and stared at the back chalkboard for a few minutes to collect her thoughts. She needed a break. Maybe she'd stop at Chase's tonight for supper at the bar. Maybe she'd rent a movie and goof off and not worry about grading papers until tomorrow. Her cell phone jarred her out of her reverie. She glanced at the caller I.D.—Joel.

"Hello?" She hadn't expected to hear from him for a while.

He sounded cheerful. "I know you're busy and I wasn't going to bother you, but it's Friday, and I started my first batch of beer in the brewery. I want to celebrate."

"What have you got in mind?"

"Steaks and baked potatoes, grilled on the patio here. A salad from a bag. I bought them on my lunch break. I'd like to show you the place."

She'd been in the dairy, couldn't imagine it as an eatery. How much had he changed it? "I'm in. I'll buy a six-pack of beer."

"I have wine."

"What time do you want me?"

"Five thirty? I have to pick up Adele and bring her here."

"I'm starving. I'll grab her and meet you at five. Does that work?"

"Even better. See you soon."

A perfect distraction. Her mood lifted. The brewery must be coming along. She couldn't wait to see it. She drove home and changed out of her school clothes into jeans and a long, loose T-shirt. She thought loose clothes disguised how thin she was. Then she drove to Daphne's stained-glass shop.

Daphne still had customers browsing in her aisles. Miriam stepped in to say hi to her.

Daphne looked her up and down. "Hmm, these days you usually leave school on Fridays, grab a sandwich, then change into your pajamas to chill at home."

Miriam grinned. "I came to pick up Adele. Joel asked me to the brewery for supper tonight. He's making steaks on his grill."

"Nice." At one time Daphne had hung out with her on Fridays, but since she'd married her chef, who worked every Friday, she went to her parents' house for supper instead. There was a time Daphne had sworn she'd never spend time with them again; they were too controlling, too narrow-minded. But Miriam knew what a blessing family could be, so she'd encouraged her to give them another chance. And her parents changed. They realized how happy Daphne was and supported her. Now, Miriam and Daphne met at Chase's bar on Thursdays.

Daphne raised an eyebrow at her. "I think Joel has a thing for you."

"Right. I'm the catch of the day."

A customer came to the counter, and Daphne laughed. She gave one last parting shot before Miriam headed upstairs to get Adele: "You'd better be careful. You might be in over your head."

"Wouldn't that be fun?" But she wasn't buying it. Who else was Joel going to ask over for supper on a Friday night? She was single and available. She trudged up the stairs and knocked on Joel's apartment door and waited for Adele to let her in. Nothing. She knocked again. Nada. The third time she pounded on the door and yelled, "Hey! Get off your ass and let me in!"

Footsteps hurried toward her. Adele cracked the door open and glanced guiltily at the TV.

Miriam shook her head. "There's a Pause button on the remote, you know."

Adele blushed. "I didn't hear you."

She let it pass. She'd watched the girl zone out more than she stayed in the real world. "Hey, your dad called me and invited the two of us to supper at the brewery. I came to pick you up."

Adele grinned, excited. "He told me, but I forgot."

"No, you didn't. You remember all kinds of stuff. You just lost track of time."

Adele didn't argue. She couldn't. She remembered birthdays and the listings for every one of her favorite TV shows and Miriam knew it. Instead, she asked, "How's he going to cook? The kitchen isn't ready."

"He's grilling. We hit the jackpot. He's making steaks."

"I love steaks!" She bit her bottom lip, worried. "I have trouble cutting them, though. Dad usually helps me."

"If he won't, I will. Come on."

Adele glanced at the TV, torn. Joel had said she was hooked, but the girl had it bad.

"Tape the end of your show. You can watch it later."

"How do I do that?"

Miriam grabbed the remote and hit the record button. "There. You can have it all. Great food. Great company. And you can finish your show when you get home."

Adele looked like she'd won the lottery. On the way down the steps, Miriam could hardly keep from grabbing her elbow to help her with her balance. "You have trouble with steps, don't you?"

"Dad usually helps me." Adele's one leg was strong, the other one weak. She looked like she could tip over any time.

"I didn't want to embarrass you. Can I help you?" Miriam asked.

"I wish you would. Dad's looking for a house for us. A ranch with no steps. He says it's safer."

Joel was right. Thankfully, her cottage's back patio opened right into the kitchen. Miriam would have gray hair if she had to watch Adele navigate stairs very often. When they reached Miriam's old Mercedes, she said, "You get to ride shotgun."

Adele laughed. "Dad always says that."

"Does he? Great minds and . . . well, you know. He's a great dad, isn't he?"

"He loves me."

Miriam looked at her. Adele had no qualms about her dad always being there for her. That was pretty damned awesome. "Well, I'm hungry. I hope he's as good a cook as he is a father."

Adele looked less sure of that. "I like his steaks, but restaurants make them better."

Miriam threw back her head and laughed. "Uh-oh, he'd better step up his game. Mill Pond is a foodie destination."

Adele frowned. "What does that mean?"

"It means everyone takes food seriously and they only cook top-notch stuff."

Adele sighed. "Dad's in trouble."

Miriam pulled onto Main Street and headed to the brewery. "Nah. Tyne will give him some tips. He'll up his game in no time."

Adele took on a dreamy look. "Tyne's cute."

"He's a hottie, for sure. But he's one happily married man. Daphne's perfect for him."

"I like Daphne."

It was easy to sidetrack Adele. Miriam started pointing out the local businesses and farms they passed. By the time they pulled to the side door of the brewery, Adele was in a good mood. She perked up more when she saw her dad tending the charcoal grill on the patio.

They parked and went to join him. Joel had three foil packets cooking over the coals. "The potatoes are about done," he told them. He reached into a cooler and brought out a bottle of sangria and a can of root beer. "You can do the honors."

Miriam passed out drinks while Joel put three thick rib-eye steaks on the grill. He seasoned them with salt, pepper, and some other kind of seasoning, then motioned to the cooler again. "The salads are in there."

"Salads?" Miriam lifted the lid and saw a bag of Caesar salad—all ingredients included—and a container of coleslaw. She saw a plastic bowl on the picnic table and emptied the Caesar salad into it. Three plastic plates, along with silverware, sat on washable placemats. Joel had thought of everything.

"Want barbecue sauce?" he asked as he flipped the steaks.

"I do!" Adele cried.

"Me too." Miriam watched him reach into the cooler for his favorite bottle of sauce. The same brand she used.

Soon, they sat at the picnic table to eat. The steaks might not rival Tyne's, but they were damned good. So were the chopped potatoes with butter and salt when she opened the foil packet. She licked her lips. "You can cook this for me anytime."

They talked about their day as they watched the sun lower in the sky.

"How much property do you own here?" Miriam asked.

Joel pointed. "All the way to the far side of the woods. I want to put a trailer near the tree line in case Miles would like to move here."

The infamous brother. Miriam remembered Joel talking about him. "And where would you like to live with Adele?"

Joel sighed. "Iris showed me some houses in town, but they all need work. I thought about buying a place on the lake, but they're hard to come by. We might have to stay in the apartment longer than I thought." He glanced at Adele, but she was fine with that.

When they finished eating, Joel motioned to a garbage can and said, "Easy cleanup. I brought these from home, but I want something better. I'm just pitching these. Adele and I need to go shopping for dishes."

Adele shrugged. Dishes obviously didn't excite her either.

Joel shook his head. "Hey, kiddo, I have something you'll be happy to see. Come on in and I'll show you what we've done."

She gave him a dubious look. He brought her here every morning and she wasn't impressed.

Miriam jumped to her feet. "How far along are you? Getting close to finished?"

"Come see." He opened the door and led them inside.

All the drywall was up and finished. The back was painted, but not the front. Miriam shook her head. "I'm not good at picturing spaces. I'd never have guessed you could have a big family room and a bigger bar area." She walked over to look at the brewery, completely in working order. "Nice."

Joel motioned across the hall to the kitchen. "It's ready for the equipment—all painted and plumbed, with the electrical outlets done." They glanced inside, then moved to a room behind the brewery. "This is my office."

Adele gave a small gasp when she glanced inside. The room was completely furnished with bookshelves on the back wall and a desk and computer nearby. It was the only room that had a ceiling.

"To block out noise," Joel said.

The front corner of the room held a cozy chair drawn up in front of a wall-mounted, flat-screen TV. A side table with a lamp sat near the chair with shelves under it that held row after row of DVDs.

Joel grinned at her. "You have your own space, hon."

She immediately dropped onto the chair and flipped on the TV.

"I take it you're going to stay here while I show Miriam the rest of the brewery?"

She didn't answer.

Joel looked at Miriam and shrugged. "Want to see the rest?"

"Sure do." In the family room she looked up at the steel beams overhead, then frowned at the cement floor. "Are you going to finish the eating areas like you did the kitchen?"

He nodded. "We're going to seal and polish it. I like its look. I'm still trying to decide how to decorate the place. Any ideas?"

She blinked, surprised. "No one ever asks me about decorating."

"Well, I am. I like your cottage. I don't want an English cozy look here, though."

She laughed. "Everything in Mill Pond is old-fashioned or cozy. It would be nice to have something modern, something bright."

He pulled out his smartphone and scrolled to some pictures he'd saved. "Like these?" One restaurant he'd saved had white walls covered with bright, bold paintings. Bright-colored chairs circled black tables with metal legs. Another restaurant's walls were each painted a different, strong color. The tables were gleaming white.

"I like both of them."

Joel smiled. "So do I. And for being a consultant, I'm going to name my first beer after you: Big M."

She didn't know what to say. It was too much, too big of a compliment. Joel had a way of making her feel special.

When she didn't respond, he asked, "Is that okay?"

"Are you kidding? It's awesome! It's . . . wow."

He led her back to the patio and reached into the cooler. With a grin, he brought out a beer for each of them. "To celebrate."

They clicked their cans together and sat at the picnic table, enjoying the evening. A blue jay called from the woods before it darted from one tree to another. Joel motioned toward it. "I should buy some peanuts and hang up a feeder. I like birds."

"So do I. I fill the feeders I hang in my sycamore tree with a variety of bird seeds—oilers, safflower seeds, and suet."

"Don't you worry about your cats? That they'll catch one of the birds you bring to your yard?"

She rolled her eyes. "They're not hunters. I got them when they were too little. Their mother hadn't taught them how to hunt. That, and they're too well-fed."

"What about instinct?"

"Their instinct is to find a spot close to the fireplace."

He chuckled and leaned forward to put his elbows on the picnic table, relaxing. "Three squares a day and a roof over my head make me pretty happy."

She snorted. "A man with simple needs."

"Hey, I've learned what's important and what's not over the years. Feeling good in your own skin and having someone to love make a big difference." He narrowed his gaze on her, and suddenly, she felt warm.

She drained her beer. She hardly ever thought about it, but right now, she wished she was curvy and petite, that she was as attractive as Daphne. "You're a pretty decent guy."

"You're a pretty decent gal. I like you."

Her mouth went dry. "I like you, too." God, they sounded like they were in high school, but she had no flirting skills. She said whatever popped into her head.

"Do you have lots of guy friends?" He'd seen her with Tyne and Chase, knew they were comfortable with each other.

"A few."

"Need another one?"

She stared. "Are you volunteering?"

"Yeah. it would be nice to have someone to do stuff with."

She felt herself relax. He'd made her nervous, but she could be a friend. She'd like someone to do stuff with, too. "Friends, I can do. I'm good at that."

"Cool." He grinned, and she realized how nice he looked when he was happy. He reached across the table and put his hand over hers. "To friendship."

At his touch, energy shot through her, catching her by surprise. She glanced at the skyline and said, "It's going to be dark soon."

He stood and gathered their beer cans to throw in the recycle bin. "I didn't realize it was so late. I really enjoyed having you here tonight. Thanks for coming for supper."

"My pleasure." She meant it. She'd had a nice night, too. "I'd better head home. I have tons to get done tomorrow."

He watched her walk to her car before going inside to get Adele. She waved good-bye as she pulled away. Why had she made such a fuss about the sun setting? What was wrong with her? Why hadn't she asked for another beer and enjoyed his company a little longer?

Miriam squirmed as she turned on the road that would take her home. She'd wanted to stay and spend time with him too much, that's why. That made her nervous. Better to play it safe than end up sorry. *Take it slow*, she told herself.

But as she pulled into her driveway and saw the cats jump in the front window to watch her walk to the door, she was already hoping Joel would call to invite her to his brewery again soon. How pitiful was that?

# Chapter 13

Joel didn't work at the brewery on weekends. Nick and the crew spent time with their families or girlfriends, and he had no desire to work alone. His parents had called and they were going to make the three-hour drive to see his new brewery and Mill Pond. They wanted the full tour—the lake, the national forest, and town. Adele was excited. His parents doted on her.

Every Saturday Joel trekked to a doughnut shop and brought home breakfast for himself and Adele. Their special treat. This morning he watched her settle in front of the TV to eat her cream-filled sub and shook his head when he brought her coffee with milk. "Don't get too comfortable. Mom and Dad will be here for lunch."

She gave a happy nod. "I'll be ready." She loved spending time with her grandparents.

Joel swept and mopped, straightening up the apartment for them to see. There'd been a time when he'd tried to teach Adele to do different chores, but the results were never good. He'd have to redo everything she did, disheartening for her and frustrating for him. Since then, he'd kept things simple. She had to unload the dishwasher and dust, and she took great pride in both of those things. Good enough.

By noon the apartment was spotless when his dad knocked on his door.

Adele threw it wide. "Grandpa! Grandma!"

They took turns hugging her.

His mom pressed both hands to Adele's cheeks, cradling her head. "It's so good to see your pretty face again."

He gave them the grand tour of the apartment—Adele's bedroom, his cramped bedroom, which was meant to be an office, the living room and kitchen. "We haven't done anything with it," he said. "We're hoping to find a house soon."

"That would be nice. Are you looking for something close to the brewery?" His mom hated to drive, had worked as a nurse in a hospital close to home so she didn't have to drive across town, but loved being a passenger. On rides she was a scenery watcher.

Joel shrugged. "Mill Pond's small enough, we could settle anywhere. We just haven't found anything suitable." He waved around the small space. "This is all there is to show you here. Ready to go to Ralph's Diner for lunch?"

They all piled into his dark green, oversize pickup, and he pointed out the different tourist shops on their drive to Ralph's.

His mom rode shotgun and Adele sat in the back with Joel's dad. His mom pointed to the different shops. "This town's so quaint. I love the awnings and flower boxes." She spent hours gardening. She had extensive flowerbeds, and every year she canned and froze a year's worth of vegetables and fruits. She'd love Miriam's English garden. Joel would have to drive past her cottage so Mom could see it.

Ralph's Diner was doing a good lunch business, but it wasn't as crowded as most weekdays. When they walked in, Ralph looked up and waved at them. Jules motioned them to a four-top. "Be with you in a minute." People nodded and smiled as they made their way to their table.

"People are nice here," Dad commented.

Adele smiled at the room in general. "Everyone likes me."

"Why wouldn't they? What's not to like?" His dad gave her a hug.

After they ordered, Mom leaned forward and winked at Adele. "Grandpa and I are going to Michigan to visit my brother for the first week of June. We were hoping your dad would drive you to our house and let you come with us."

Adele's jaw dropped. She turned to Joel. "Can I?"

"We've missed seeing her," his mom added. "We'd like to spend some time with her."

Joel's uncle owned ten acres and raised a few cattle. He had lots of dogs and cats that roamed in and out of the barn. Adele loved visiting there. Joel would be extra busy then, trying to finish things up at the brewery. He shrugged. "How can I say no?"

Adele squeaked her pleasure, and for the rest of the meal, the talk turned to Uncle Russell and his farm. As they talked, it occurred to

Joel that Miriam would be finished teaching seniors by June. He'd have a week of free nights. Maybe he could invite her to suppers more often. Maybe . . . but he tamped down that thought. He'd better not get ahead of himself.

When they finished eating, he said, "Come on. Let me give you the grand tour of Mill Pond."

First, he drove them toward the national forest. On their way, they passed Mill Pond High and Art's Grocery, then they turned toward Tyne and Daphne's log cabin.

"They invited us to their house for supper," Adele explained.

Joel followed the highway to Harley's winery and then circled the lake all the way to Ian's resort. When they passed Miriam's house, he pointed out her perennial flowerbeds and, as he'd suspected, his mother oohed and aahed over them.

"Miriam has two cats," Adele told them. "They like me."

It was a straight shot from there past Miriam's parents' house.

"Miriam invited us there for their Sunday get-together," Adele said.

"Sounds like the town's greeted you with open arms. Most small towns are cliquish. I was a little worried about that," his dad said.

"Mill Pond is special. People help one another." When Joel pulled to the side door of the brewery, he turned to his parents with pride. "Well, this is it."

Joel's dad liked the side patio with its umbrellaed tables. "Reminds me of our root beer stand back home. A good place to grab a dog and something cold."

Joel led them inside and they gushed over what he'd accomplished. They were that kind of parents, always supportive.

His dad scratched his head at the cement floors. "Who'd have thought you could make concrete look this polished and nice?"

His mom liked his office with the cozy nook for Adele. "You'll feel better having her with you."

Once he'd explained how he hoped the business would work, he led them back outside and pointed to the woods in the distance. He'd had a foundation poured close to the tree line. "I mean to put a trailer there, in case Miles ever needs a place to stay."

His dad's lips thinned. "Your brother's not your responsibility. You have enough to take care of."

Joel knew he meant Adele, but he shook his head. "I don't want him to move back in with you guys. It's time you two start having some fun."

His mom turned her head and swiped at her eyes. "We do have fun. I have my gardens and your dad likes his job."

Joel's dad refilled vending machines, driving from one place to another to keep them stocked. At sixty, he'd worked for the company long enough to have a decent pension if he retired, but he wanted to wait until he was sixty-five and could apply for Medicare. In the evenings he puttered in the garage on an old muscle car that was his pride and joy. When Joel and Miles had lived at home, they'd spent lots of evenings out there, handing him tools and yakking. His mom had worked Monday through Wednesdays, twelve-hour shifts, as a nurse until she was fifty-five. They had friends galore, and they'd been there for Miles every time he crashed. His brother hadn't been an alcoholic when he joined the army, but he'd hit the bottle hard when he came home.

His dad ran his hand through his hair. It was thick and wavy, a source of pride for him. "Worths don't go bald," he'd told Joel often. He let out a long breath of air. "Your brother's to the point that he either wants to get better or he doesn't. He might not be able to kick his habit."

"I know. I'm just offering him a place to stay, and maybe a job."

"A job?" His dad sounded worried.

"Custodial work, like he's doing now. Nothing fancy. If he doesn't show up for work, I'll have to hire someone else."

His dad's shoulders relaxed. That seemed to mollify him a little.

His mom looked at where the trailer would be, the setting. "It's beautiful here."

Joel nodded. "I think Miles will like it. My hope is that he keeps the job he has, but if something happens . . ." They all knew what that would be. Miles would drink himself into a stupor, lose three or four days and not show up for work. "Well, then he can come here."

"It might work," his dad said. "No guarantees."

"There are no guarantees with Miles." His mom said it softly, as though she hated saying the words.

Joel wouldn't push it. He'd thrown it out there and he'd let them adjust to the idea. He cleared his throat. "Well, you've seen the works. What do you think of Mill Pond?"

"I think you've found someplace special." His mom slipped her arm through Adele's. "And you live close enough that we can come and grab our granddaughter every once in a while to keep track of her. I think it's perfect."

"I was thinking about taking you to Chase's for supper," Joel said. "It's a bar, but he makes great burgers, and he has an outdoor patio where kids can eat."

Adele stuck out her bottom lip.

"What is it, hon?" his mom asked.

"One of my favorite TV shows is on tonight."

Joel was about to tell her to tape the show, she could watch it later, but his mom grinned. "Good, you and I can grab something to eat and stay in to chat. We'll have some girl time together."

"Once she turns on the TV . . ."

His mom cut him off. "I know. We'll watch the show together."

He knew better than to argue with his mom. She was the kindest person in the world, but when it came to Adele, she wouldn't bend. If she wanted to stay in and watch TV with her, that's what she'd do. He gave his daughter a look she ignored. He'd talk to her later, but it wouldn't make a lot of difference. By the time this happened again, she'd forget anything he'd told her.

His dad lay his hand on Joel's shoulder. "It's you and me, kid. Let's drop the girls off and go for burgers and beer."

Joel gave in gracefully. He stopped at Art's Grocery and let his mom buy fancy cheeses and meats to make toasted sandwiches. Then he dropped them at his apartment and he and his dad headed to Chase's.

Because Adele wasn't with them, they went inside to eat. Miriam and Daphne were sitting at a table and waved them over. Joel introduced his dad and that was all it took. His dad loved to yak. He turned on the charm, and from then on, Joel never got a word in. When their food came, he happily munched and listened to the ebb and flow of conversation.

Miriam asked what Joel had been like as a kid.

"Kindhearted. Always busy. The kid couldn't sit still."

"A good student?"

His dad laughed. "He did well enough."

She cocked an eyebrow in Joel's direction. "Not studious."

He shrugged and locked gazes with her. "I was no A student, but I've always been good with my hands." When she blushed, he smirked.

Miriam turned her attention back to his dad. "When did you start working for the vending company?"

"Right out of high school. You could do that back then, get a good job with a high school diploma. And you had security, a job for life." He shook his head. "Things have changed."

"So, what sells out first in your machines?" Daphne asked. "Candy? Cakes?"

"Chips, for sure," his dad said.

"I love chips." Miriam reached for Joel's last fry. "Any kind of potatoes really."

Daphne glanced at their empty plates. "Tyne loves to ask what you'd have for your last meal, if you could have anything. You?" She looked at Joel's dad.

"A standing rib roast—the whole thing."

Daphne laughed. "Miriam?"

"Easy. You said a meal, right? A bacon cheeseburger with fries and a banana split for dessert."

Daphne turned to Joel.

"Cabbage rolls with a baked potato and apple pie."

His dad smiled and shook his head. "Your mom makes that every year for your birthday."

"She says it's perfect for January, brings us good luck."

Miriam studied him, serious. "You're a Capricorn?"

"Yup, the sign of the goat."

"The sea goat," she corrected. "And hard work. I'm going to learn to make cabbage rolls for you."

Daphne looked surprised. So did Joel. "It's a pain in the rear to make. That's why Mom only makes it once a year."

"I'll only make it once a year, too, but I'm going to ask Tyne to show me how."

When his dad raised an eyebrow, Daphne said, "Tyne's my husband, a chef."

"I'll tell you what." His dad pointed a finger at Miriam. "My wife guards that recipe, but if you're serious, I'll have her give it to you since you're making it for our boy."

She blinked. "You'd do that?"

"Damn straight."

Chase came with their checks and Joel picked up the tabs and paid them. Then they all stood to leave.

"Thanks for the supper," the girls told Joel. They separated in the parking lot, and when Joel and his dad started back to his apartment, his dad gave him a thumbs-up. "I like her."

"Which one?"

"Your Miriam. She's solid."

Joel shook his head. "She's not mine. We're just friends."

"For now." His dad smiled. "Whatever recipe that girl wants, she can have."

Once they reached the apartment, his parents didn't linger long.

"We have a long drive home, but this was nice. We'll do it again," his mom said. "And in a couple of weeks you'll bring us Adele and we'll take off for vacation."

If they'd take Adele for a week or two every once in a while, it would be nice.

There might be advantages to not living close to his parents, Joel decided. He loved his daughter, but he rarely had free time. Now, he would.

# Chapter 14

Miriam went to her family's Sunday meal, as usual, but after they ate and finished dessert, when her nephews started to sign people up for Wiffle ball, she had to decline. "Too many papers to grade, damn it. I worked on them all day yesterday."

"That's not what I heard." Her sister, Sue-Ellen, who was sitting across from her, smirked. Her auburn hair was pulled into a frizzy topknot today, with tiny strands breaking free to curl around her face. "Sally Coleridge was at Chase's bar last night with her husband and saw you having supper with Daphne and that nice man you brought here one Sunday."

"Joel." Miriam looked around the table, ready to defend herself. "He brought his dad to Chase's and we invited them to sit with us. His parents drove down from Fort Wayne to see how his brewery was coming along."

Sue-Ellen's smirk grew wider and she winked at her mom at the end of the table. "Well, Miriam should know about that. News is, Joel took her to his place and grilled steaks for her there."

Miriam rolled her eyes. There were no secrets in Mill Pond. "He's lonely. He wants a friend."

Sue-Ellen's husband, Neil, broke in. "You gotta give the guy credit. Most men his age want someone ten years younger hanging on their arm."

Miriam wrinkled her nose. "I don't get it. What would they have in common?"

Her dad grunted. "I don't think the guys are worried about deep conversations."

"Well, they should be." Her mom pushed to her feet, ready to clear the dessert plates. "Sex is great and all, but it won't hold you together when things get tough. Raising kids, paying the mortgage, getting too tired . . . they all take their toll. Then you have to have something more to glue you together." She pointed to Sue-Ellen's boys. "Remember that, you two."

Toby, the fifteen-year-old, snickered. "People don't have to have babies these days. I had sex education this year."

"Good, then hopefully they taught you the emotions that go along with getting it on."

Toby frowned. "They taught us about the diseases."

Neil wagged a finger at him. "You come home with one of those, and so help me, I'll Super Glue your thing to your thigh."

"Dad!" Toby looked horrified.

Sue-Ellen cut in. "Some people just say no and don't have to worry about sex. Some people wait until they're married. And some people decide never to have rug rats." She nodded at Clair, sitting next to her husband, Max. "Then you can honeymoon for as long as you want."

A flush colored Clair's face. "I went off the Pill ten months ago. If something happens, fine. If not, that's fine, too."

Sue-Ellen blinked. "Our baby sister might have a baby?"

Max put a hand over Clair's. "We're not going to work at it, but if Clair gets pregnant, we'd sure be happy."

"Kids are game changers," Neil warned. "No sleep, no sex."

"Sex isn't everything," Mom repeated, her tone sharp.

Miriam got that. But boy, would she love to have a few wild and wanton rolls in the sack before she got too old and dried up.

Her mother raised an eyebrow at her. *Could she read her thoughts?* "You." She pointed to the door. "Get out of here and finish grading your papers. And if you see your nice Joel, tell him we said hi."

"Will do." Miriam stood, anxious to flee this conversation.

"As for the rest of you," Mom motioned toward the kitchen, "we have dishes to clean."

The boys started whining. "Will we play Wiffle ball when we're done?"

Miriam's dad intervened. "We'll pick teams after we finish up in here."

Everyone stood to take their places in the Sunday assembly line and Miriam got out while the getting was good. On the drive home her thoughts turned to Joel. Her family sure liked him, and so did she. What would he be like in bed? Lost in her musings, she almost didn't notice the car pulled to the side of the road. She glanced at it just when the passenger door flew open and Maya scrambled out of it. She slammed the door behind her. Tears streaked her face and T. J.'s car peeled away.

What the hell?

Miriam decided to pull on to the next turnoff to go back to check on her. Before she reached her, though, a pickup slowed and stopped by the girl. Its door opened, and Nick Hillegard walked over to her. He leaned forward, trying to help her, but Maya couldn't stop crying. He didn't know what to do. When he saw Miriam's car coming, he stepped into the road to wave her down.

"She's sad," he said. "She just keeps crying."

"I'll try to talk to her. Thanks for stopping, Nick."

He looked relieved, got back in his truck, and pulled away.

Miriam turned to Maya. "Need a ride? I can take you to the resort."

Wordlessly, Maya climbed into the old Mercedes. She only had five more days of school and then she could completely avoid T.J. if she wanted to. Seniors got out a week early. "You okay?" Miriam asked.

She knew better than to pry. When a kid wants to talk, she will. When she doesn't, it's a waste of time.

Maya's hands curled into fists. In a terse voice, she spurted, "I had sex with T. J. It was the pits. It hurt and it was over in ten minutes. When I wasn't happy, he was ready to take me home. He's going to hang out with his friends the rest of the day."

Miriam cringed. "T. J. didn't do anything to make the experience good for you?"

"I don't think he knows how to." She wiped at her eyes. "When I told him that, he got mad at me."

"You told him?" Miriam didn't think most girls would complain about T. J. rolling around with them in the backseat of his car, whether he was any good or not. Miriam's worry bubbled to the surface. "Condom?" she asked.

"No, Hazel took me to get the Shot. That made T. J. happy. No worries for him."

Thank God for Paula's mother. At least Maya wouldn't get pregnant. Miriam tried to comfort her. "Guys and girls don't think of sex the same way. Guys just want it. Girls read something into it."

"Well, T. J. can read something into ours—a big, fat good-bye."

Miriam glanced at her. T. J. probably wasn't used to a tough critic. She'd underestimated the girl. "I'm proud of you. Every girl needs to respect herself."

Maya turned to her with a flinty expression on her face. "No worries there. I just wanted someone to love me. No one ever has."

"You know sex isn't the same as love, right?"

Maya shrugged. "T. J. kept saying he loved me, but he's not very good at it."

Miriam almost felt sorry for the boy. The first time she'd gone to bed with a guy in college, neither of them had had any experience. They'd fumbled their way to a climax. But Miriam didn't want Maya to be with T. J. She wanted her to start college, so she said, "Paula and Hazel love you. I care about you."

"You guys are the best. I know that, but it's different, you know? I wanted to be special to someone."

"It'll happen," Miriam said. "Just give it time."

"How much time?"

A good question. It still hadn't happened for her.

# Chapter 15

Joel drove Adele to work with him, as usual, on Monday. This time, though, she was going to stay the entire day. While the men worked on finishing the cement floor in the bar, she'd camp out in the office in her private sitting area.

At lunchtime they drove into town and ate at Ralph's Diner.

"We only have a couple more weeks of work." Nick motioned to his crew. "We're going to miss your free lunches when we finish this job."

Adele frowned. "Won't we still come here?"

"No; enjoy it while you can," Joel warned Adele. "Once the brewery opens for business, we won't have time to leave the building."

Her face fell. "But I like it here."

"Then we'll come once a week for supper, but soon, you'll be sitting in the brewery, chowing down on hot dogs and root beer."

"Every day?"

That would get old after a while. "There's a microwave in the office. We could pack you something from home sometimes. And there'll be bowls of chili. Tyne said I should double the ground beef and punch up half of it to put nachos on the menu." Easy enough. Just flavored hamburger over chips with shredded cheese and lettuce on top. Joel wasn't offering gourmet.

Nick finished his meat loaf and potatoes. "I'll have to pack my lunches again, but this has been fun while it lasted."

Joel had enjoyed working with Nick and his crew, too. He was about to say so when a young woman came to join them at their table. She was pretty enough, with long, auburn hair and an hourglass figure, but her dark eyes glittered boldly. When she smiled at Nick, he sat up straighter and looked wary.

"Hey, Chantelle, congratulations."

She gave him a sour look and turned her attention to Joel. When she didn't see a ring on his finger, she raised her eyebrows at Nick. "You have a new friend?"

"Me and my crew are working for him. This is Joel Worth and his daughter, Adele."

"You're the guy who bought the dairy to open as a microbrewery?"

"That's the plan."

Her full lips curled in a seductive smile. "Store owners turn me on."

Sure they did. So did their money. He didn't want anything to do with her and had a pretty good idea how to sidetrack her. He smiled, too. "When's your baby due?"

Her look went sour again. "Too soon. I'm not ready to be a mom."

"My first wife felt the same way. That's why we went our separate ways. But you might surprise yourself when you hold the baby for the first time."

"I don't see that happening, but Eddie's excited about it."

"At least someone wants the baby." Joel didn't hide his sarcasm.

She grimaced and stood. "When your brewery's done, I'll have to come check it out."

"You shouldn't drink in your condition."

She snorted. "Yeah right."

They watched her leave, and Adele turned to her father. She looked surprised. "You weren't nice to her."

"I didn't like her."

"But you're nice to everybody."

How could he explain? "She'd want to be friends, and I don't want to be friends with her."

"Because of me?"

Joel stared. "No, it doesn't have anything to do with you."

"You moved here to get away from Mom because she always made me sad."

"That was only part of it."

"Did you think Chantelle would make me sad?"

Joel took a long breath. People at neighboring tables were trying hard not to listen in, but how could they miss their conversation? "I thought she'd make both of us sad."

Nick intervened. "Your dad's right. Chantelle was only interested in him because he has money."

Adele's jaw dropped. "Mom was always asking Dad for more money, too."

Joel nodded. "Chantelle would be a lot like your mom. I can't go through that again."

Adele reached out to place her crippled hand over his. "I understand."

And Joel realized that she did. "Thanks, hon."

She beamed, happy with herself, and Nick patted her on the shoulder. "Good job, kid. I feel like dessert today. What about a brownie delight?"

Adele loved rich desserts, and soon they were making their way through scoops of ice cream and whipping cream to reach a fudge brownie drowned in hot fudge sauce. By the time they finished eating, she'd forgotten about Chantelle.

When they returned to the brewery after lunch, Adele shut herself in her private sanctuary to watch the old movie *Seven Brides for Seven Brothers*, and Joel knew she'd be humming and happy at the end of the day. The movie had lots of singing and dancing and romance—all of her favorites. While the cement floor dried in the bar, Joel went to help Nick and his crew finish painting the primed walls in the family room. He'd decided to make the long outside walls bright canary yellow; the front wall, cobalt blue; and the inside wall, fire engine red.

Nick's brows furrowed in a troubled frown while he painted.

"What's bugging you?" Joel asked. "You don't like my color choices?"

"Love 'em." He hesitated. "Do you remember Roxy, the girl I met in Indy?"

"The party girl?"

Nick's frown deepened. "Yeah, well; she asked to borrow some money from me this weekend. She's having a tough time."

Joel stopped to dip his roller in the paint tray and glanced at Nick. "Did you give it to her?"

"It wasn't that much, only a few hundred."

"Will she pay you back?"

Nick didn't answer right away. "I doubt it."

"Then it wasn't a loan. Are you all right with that?"

"I was until now. That's why Chantelle hit on you at the diner. She wanted a sugar daddy."

*Sugar daddy.* He hadn't heard those words for a while. Joel chose his answer carefully. "When I met April, I knew all she wanted was someone to take care of her. And money. I thought she'd love me if I came through for her, but it didn't work that way. Even after we got married, that's all she wanted from me. I don't want to do that to my-self again."

Nick grimaced. "I'm getting played, aren't I?"

"It's possible. Everyone falls on tough times, so I don't know for sure, but it's something to think about."

"April played you, right?"

"Big-time."

"Shit." Nick finished his section of the wall and stepped back to examine it. He sighed. "I don't want to get screwed over by some girl. She always has enough money to go out."

"Then be smart; ask yourself questions and listen to your gut. Test the waters. Tell her your money's going to be tight pretty soon be-cause you're investing in building your business and see how she re-acts. April liked me a lot less when I had less disposable income."

Nick seemed to like that idea. He nodded. "Thanks, man."

"We all learn from our mistakes if we don't want to repeat them."

Nick ran a hand through his wavy brown hair. "Girls get played, too, I guess." He told Joel about stopping to comfort Maya on the side of the road. "She was crying so hard, I didn't know what to do until Miriam got there."

That made Joel worry. He thought about meeting Chantelle at the diner, unhappy and pregnant. Maya was on the Pill, wasn't she? "If anyone can help the girl, it's Miriam." He finished painting, too, and stepped back to look for any spots he'd missed.

"It looks good," Nick said. "I think our wall's done."

And soon, the crew finished the walls they'd been working on, too. Joel was sure he'd like them once they dried. If they got lucky, the floor in the bar would be set enough that they could paint in there the next day. They'd be ready to install appliances and light fixtures next week.

"Might as well call it a day," Nick said. "We'll meet you back here tomorrow."

Joel was only working with them in the morning tomorrow. The rest of the day, he was training the new help he'd hired—all but the cook. First, he needed a stove and a grill, but he wasn't worried about Dave. He'd been the line cook at the plastics factory before it closed its doors.

It was earlier than usual, so Joel went to collect Adele to drive home. They'd eaten out enough lately that he craved real food for supper. When he'd looked in the refrigerator this morning, he hadn't seen anything to brag about. "Let's stop at the grocery store and grab a few things," he said.

"Can we have chicken?"

He knew what Adele was asking for. One of her favorite meals was chicken breasts breaded in crushed potato chips. He'd made it for her since she was a little girl. "Why not? We'll buy some sides, too."

On the way to Art's, he decided to call Miriam and invite her for supper, too. He got her voice mail and said, "Nick told me about Maya. I'm curious about how she's doing, how you're doing. I know you like the girl."

He was buying a bag of shredded cabbage and carrots to make coleslaw when Miriam called back. "I'll be there."

"My place. Five o'clock? Nothing fancy."

"Sounds good."

He bought some rice in a bag and a jar of dressing for the slaw. On a whim, he threw in a tub of ice cream, too. Adele added a jar of hot fudge and grinned at him.

By the time Miriam came at five, everything was ready. She glanced around their apartment, unimpressed. Why would she be? There was nothing on the walls. Most of their possessions were still in boxes.

"We're only staying here short-term," he said. "Once the brewery's finished, I'd like to find a house."

She sat down with Adele at the small, round dining table near the kitchen. "Iris has been complaining that there aren't a lot of houses for sale right now. She doesn't have many showings."

He carried the hot pans to the table and set them on trivets. He handed Miriam a serving spoon to dish up. "I don't really want to build a house. That takes a lot of time and attention."

She frowned at the chicken. "What's this?"

Adele answered. "He coats chicken with potato chips for me."

Miriam put two breasts on her plate, then reached to scoop out some rice. She raised her eyebrows. "You made coleslaw?"

"Sort of. I bought a bag and some dressing and mixed them together."

She took a taste. "It's good."

She really *wasn't* a cook. Tyne would be expecting something exotic with caraway seeds, but there was nothing fancy about the food Joel made. It kept them fed, though.

Miriam tried the chicken. "*Mmm*, I like this."

Yup, no class at all. Like him. He grinned. "Glad you like it. So, how's your Maya? Is everything okay with her?"

She explained while they finished their meal. When the ice cream was gone, he loaded the last bowls and spoons in the dishwasher and tried to think how to keep Miriam there longer.

Adele came up with the answer. "Want to play a game of Life? It's more fun with three people."

Why that appealed to Miriam, he didn't know. He'd played the game plenty of times with Adele, but to say that he enjoyed it would be pushing it. *She* enjoyed it, though, so that was enough. To his surprise, Miriam really got into it, hooting each time Joel drew a crappy card. He ended up losing, with a car full of five kids and lots of debt. Miriam won and loved it.

"You like to gloat, don't you?" he said.

"In case you didn't notice, my family's competitive. Don't play poker with me or you'll lose your shirt."

He raised his eyebrows in a challenge. "Maybe I'd like that."

Her blue eyes blazed. "I've always wanted to play strip poker."

Adele laughed and Miriam blushed. The words had popped out before she'd monitored them. "You like to tease, like Dad does."

Miriam looked relieved. Adele had only sort of gotten what she'd said. She knew it was a joke, though.

Joel grinned. "Anytime you're up for a serious game, let me know."

Miriam narrowed her eyes, studying him. "I might take you up on that."

"Then get ready to lose, because some things motivate me more than others."

She laughed, and the night ended on an upbeat note.

When Miriam left and Adele went to bed, Joel replayed their conversation in his mind. He'd drive Adele to his parents' house on Saturday, and Miriam's load at school would be lighter after the seniors' last day this Friday. Could a game of strip poker be in his future?

# Chapter 16

Miriam tried to concentrate during her free period, but she'd felt unsettled all day. Friday would be the end of school for the seniors. Was that what was setting her on edge? She'd have all their term papers to grade, but she'd have more time next week without the two senior English classes she taught. She'd easily get her paperwork caught up. Her mind kept drifting to Joel and she'd push those thoughts away. Had he been serious last night or just teasing her? He didn't strike her as the strip poker type.

"Miss Reinhardt?" Maya raised her voice, and Miriam jerked to attention.

"Sorry, my mind drifted."

"I know you're probably busy, but I was hoping I could talk to you."

"Sure, pull up a chair."

Maya settled across from her and grimaced. "I might have waited too long, but I was wondering if I could still get a scholarship to IU. I've saved enough money to buy myself a car, and I can drive back and forth for classes and still work with Hazel at the day care to make pocket money."

*Hallelujah! The girl had finally come to her senses.* "I'll call the counselor I worked with to let her know. She's been holding a place for you as a favor to me. We've worked together for a long time."

Maya let out a relieved sigh. "I was afraid . . ."

Miriam waved the words away. "We've already listed all the classes you want to take. Some of them might have filled up, but we have plenty of time to choose other ones."

Maya pushed to her feet. "Thank you for not giving up on me."

"Not until I had to. Congratulations, Maya. You'll be a student at IU this fall."

The girl's face lit up with a smile, and Miriam felt like jumping up and dancing around the room. She hated watching potential go to waste. The happy glow stayed with her to the end of the day. She rolled down the windows of her car and sang along to the radio on the drive home. Tommy and Tuppence picked up on her mood when she walked in the cottage and jumped on her lap for extra lovies.

After she gave them lots of attention, she grabbed a beer and walked out to her backyard to look at the lake. When her cell phone rang, she answered it with a lilt in her voice. She always enjoyed talking to her little sister.

"Hey, Clair! What's new?"

There was a slight pause and then the words gushed out. "I'm pregnant!"

Miriam couldn't hold in the happy squeal that bubbled inside her. "Congratulations! Oh my gosh, I'm so happy for you!" She bit her bottom lip to keep from babbling.

"Everyone's coming to celebrate. Get your ass over here!"

"I'm on my way." She changed into jeans and a loose T-shirt, then made the drive to her sister's house on the far side of the lake. Her mom and dad's car was already parked next to Neil and Sue-Ellen's. People were in the front yard, hugging and laughing. Clair's husband, Max, was pumping everyone's hands. When she walked toward them, Max turned to her and wrapped her in a bear hug.

Miriam laughed. Max was usually more reticent than Clair. She'd never seen him this happy. "You're going to be a dad!"

He flushed with happiness. "It's great, isn't it?"

"It's awesome."

Her mom disappeared inside the long, shingled, ranch-style house and came out with a platter of burgers for Dad to put on the grill. Their family never got together without food. Sue-Ellen had brought bags of chips and dips. Miriam, as usual, carried in the beer and beverages.

Sue-Ellen's boys kept slapping each other on the back. "There'll be a baby at Christmas this year."

Miriam felt proud of them. Most teenage boys would be leery of a newborn.

"How long before we can babysit?" Toby asked.

"You can't pass the kid around like a football," Sue-Ellen warned.

Sam rolled his eyes. "We know that. If we babysit, Clair will pay us, though, won't she?"

So that was it. Miriam's nephews were always looking for ways to make money. She had to give them credit, though; when she hired them to do a job, they didn't monkey around. She'd had them clean her flowerbeds and yard last fall, and they'd done it better than she did. All her neighbors hired them to do small jobs around their houses.

When the burgers were ready, they pulled their lawn chairs in a circle and sat with their paper plates balanced on their knees, yakking.

"You have the perfect house for kids," Mom said. "Two bedrooms and a bathroom on one end and two bedrooms and a bath on the other. When they're little, you can keep the kids close, and when they're older, you can move them across the house and have a little privacy."

Max kept reaching for Clair's hand and smiled every time he touched her.

"How do you feel?" Miriam asked. "Any nausea?"

"Never felt better," Clair said. "No cravings, but I'm hungry all the time."

Max nodded. "We've had to almost double the groceries we buy."

Neil laughed. "Sue-Ellen got big as a barn with Sam, ate everything in sight, but lost all the weight and more once he was born."

Her mom nodded. "All you do is chase kids. You don't have time to finish a meal."

It was close to eight when people started to leave, and Miriam was trying not to yawn as she said her good-byes.

Clair hugged her close. "Thanks for being happy for me, Sis."

Miriam shook her head. "Why wouldn't I be? You have a great husband and now you're starting a great family."

"It's just that . . . you never wanted kids, did you?"

"Oh, you sweetie, you were worried about me, weren't you? No need. I'd rather teach other peoples' kids than have my own."

Clair's shoulders relaxed. "That's what I always thought, but then I started to worry . . ."

"Don't. I'm happy for you, but it's not my thing. Hell, you can't take a summer break from your own kids, can you?"

Clair laughed. "Nope, that's not considered good parenting."

Miriam shrugged. "There you have it, then. I'll stick with Tommy and Tuppence."

Max wrapped his arm around Clair's shoulders as they stood in the front yard and waved good-bye.

On the drive home, Miriam thought about Clair's question more carefully. Did she want kids? Ever? But she didn't have any doubts. She'd rather teach than mother. If she had to deal with students all day long, the last thing she wanted was to go home to kids of her own. She wouldn't have anything to give them. She left school drained most days. Then, for no particular reason, her thoughts turned to Joel and Adele.

That would be different, wouldn't it? Adele was nineteen. True, she didn't act it, but all the raising had been done already, hadn't it? And Joel had done a great job. The serious work would be behind her. Would Adele get on her nerves if she lived with her day in and day out? Not really. Maybe a little. But not that much.

Then Miriam shook her head. What the hell was she worrying about? Joel had been through one disastrous marriage. It wasn't likely he'd try again. But if they spent a lot of time together, as friends, Adele was a welcome addition as far as she was concerned.

As she pulled in her own driveway, though, she realized she'd better start thinking about the present. Two cats sat in her front window, glaring at her. She'd left them ... again. If she were smart, she'd go in there and jolly them up. Which sounded like a great game plan to her.

The rest of the night, she cuddled on the couch, watching TV with Tommy on one side of her and Tuppence on the other. Between students and cats, she felt complete.

# Chapter 17

On Wednesday Joel and Nick and the entire crew concentrated on finishing the cement floor in the family room so it looked like brick. Adele, as usual, watched TV in her tiny sanctum, ignoring them.

It took them the entire day, only breaking for lunch at Ralph's, to complete the project. Nick looked it over and gave a low whistle. "This would work great in my sister's basement."

"You have a sister?" It was the first Joel had heard about her.

"Yeah. She's a nurse in Bloomington. Married a physical therapist who works there, too. They bought an old farmhouse that needs some TLC, but Brian and I are helping them with it."

"I bet she appreciates that."

"Oh, yeah, Heidi's pretty cool. Brian and I have always looked out for her."

Joel figured Nick was probably wrapped around her little finger. The kid had lots of charm, was plenty smart but had a soft heart. Some women would appreciate that and some would take advantage of it. Nick had better smarten up. "No kids?" he asked.

"Not yet. She's younger than I am, only twenty-five."

"Are you driving to Indy tomorrow?"

Nick nodded. "I'm in the middle of flipping a house and I'm going to tell Roxy I have to start being more careful with my money. We'll see how that plays out. If she bails or balks at it, I'd rather know now."

"Good move." Nick was a quick learner; Joel had to give him that.

Nick started packing up his tools to head home. The rest of the crew had already gone. "I'm going to have a lazy Friday night, nothing exciting, so I can get an early start tomorrow."

"We have an early start tomorrow, too," Joel said. "I'm driving Adele to my parents' place and then they're heading to my uncle's home in Michigan for a week." He hesitated. "I'm going to be lazy and grab pizza tonight for supper. Want to come with us? We might get there early enough to beat the crowd."

Nick looked surprised but nodded. "Sounds good to me. Then I can go home and watch a little TV before I crash."

They decided to drive separately; then they could head in different directions after they ate. The parking lot was already filling up, and when they walked inside, they got the last round table for four.

Nick glanced around and shook his head. "More and more tourists are hanging out here on Friday nights. The season started earlier than usual this year. When the weather turns nice, weekends get crazy with people heading to the national forest."

The waitress was coming to take their orders when a young woman stepped through the door and looked around for a place to sit. No open tables. Nick waved her to theirs. He looked at Joel. "This is Meg. She helps her dad run the hardware store in town. Meg, this is Joel Worth and his daughter, Adele."

The girl gave a friendly nod. She wore her wavy blond hair cropped short and was so pretty, the short cut accentuated her fine features. Tall and willowy, she didn't bother with makeup, not that it mattered. She didn't need any.

"I went to school with Meg's big sister, Maddie." Nick's voice sounded tight. "She went to Purdue to study engineering, then got married and moved to the East Coast."

He kept glancing at Meg as he talked, and Joel got the feeling Nick had had a crush either on her or on her sister. He couldn't decide which. Was Maddie the girl he'd meant to settle down with in Mill Pond before she left for college?

The waitress took their order, and Nick and Meg decided to split a large, super supreme. The way he talked to her made it clear he must have had a thing for Maddie and still saw Meg as the tag-along little sister. The waitress brought their drinks, then Joel turned to her. "What made you decide to stay in Mill Pond?" Surely she could have gone to college, too.

The girl's expression crumpled. "My dad had a stroke and someone had to help him run the business or he'd have lost it. I decided to stay."

"I'm so sorry." What had he been thinking? "I didn't mean to bring up something that personal."

She shrugged. "How could you know? You're new here. My mom's a bookkeeper for a few of the small businesses in town. She couldn't do that and run the store, so I started pitching in. Found out I really like it."

Nick reached over to tousle her hair. "She's a natural."

The expressions that crossed Meg's face made Joel hesitate. Happiness that Nick praised her. And frustration. That surprised him. Then Joel finally got it. Meg had a crush on Nick, but in his mind, she was always the kid sister. Joel shook his head. Meg was worth a dozen Roxys. He hoped Nick would wake up someday and see that Meg had grown up.

# Chapter 18

Joel woke Adele at eight thirty on Saturday morning. "Rise and shine, hon. We drive to Grandma and Grandpa's today."

He'd already gone to the bakery and had her favorite doughnuts and coffee waiting for her in the kitchen. He knew she'd stayed up later than usual last night, watching a midnight sales special on QVC. His daughter loved fancy dolls and had boxes of them, waiting for a place in their new home.

She glanced at him nervously when she sat across from him. "I bought a new doll last night."

He raised an eyebrow. "You did?"

"Mary, Mary, Quite Contrary," she said. "She's part of the collection I started."

He'd bought her Little Bo Peep for Christmas last year to add to Little Miss Muffet. He wondered how many kids even read nursery rhymes these days, but Adele had always loved them. The dolls were high-quality pieces with hand-painted porcelain faces. "Have you kept track of how much money you've spent this month?"

She nodded. He gave her a monthly allowance on her credit card, and when she ran out of money, she had to wait until the beginning of the next month. "I had enough," she told him.

"Then you're in good shape. Wednesday's the beginning of June." She'd get more money then. He wanted her to have some personal freedom and to learn to keep track of her own finances. The credit card worked for them.

She smiled. "The doll will get here before I get back from my trip."

"Good, then it will be waiting for you. I'll put the box in your room." That would give her something to look forward to when she got back.

They finished their breakfast and he motioned to the clock. "Better get ready to go." His cell phone rang while Adele took a quick shower and got dressed.

Miriam rushed into speech. "Hey, glad I caught you before you left. You've been nice enough to feed me lately, so I thought I'd return the favor. Want to come to my place for supper?"

"Tonight?" He had a three-hour drive to Fort Wayne and three more hours back. He'd be ready to flop on the couch and relax, but there was no way he'd turn down Miriam. "I won't get back until after six. Is that okay?"

"Yeah. I can get some stuff done that way." She sounded nervous. "I'll see you then."

He was about to say not to worry about anything fancy, that he'd probably eat a big lunch with his parents, but she hung up too fast. She wasn't going to try to cook, was she? Was that why she was nervous? Of did she have something else on her mind?

On the drive to Fort Wayne, he popped Adele's favorite CD in the player and they sang along when they knew the words. The scenery was worth the trip. Crab trees burst with white and pink blooms. Late tulips, lilacs, and irises blossomed. The three-hour drive flew by.

His parents were happy to see them. "We thought we might go to your favorite Mexican restaurant for lunch," his mom said. "Have you missed it?"

He had. He loved their spicy beef chimichangas and guacamole. By the time they'd finished eating, he felt happy but stuffed. He stayed to visit a couple more hours before he made the return trip to Mill Pond. "Have a great time in Michigan," he called as he waved good-bye.

"You have a good time, too!" His dad gave him a thumbs-up.

Good lord, were his parents worried about him? Did they think he'd turn into a lonely old hermit?

It was a little after six when he pulled into Miriam's driveway. Her cats had jumped into the front window when they heard his car. He started toward the house, then stopped and wrinkled his nose. The front door was open and the screen let a breeze from the lake blow through the cottage. What was that awful smell?

Miriam yanked the screened door open and motioned him back to his pickup. "You can't come in. I'll pay for supper if you drive us to Ralph's."

He couldn't stop a smirk. "You burned it, didn't you?"

Her corkscrew curls stood on end, as if she'd run her hands through them too many times. She tossed a dirty look his way. "I wanted to surprise you. I tried to make cabbage rolls. Nothing went right. I burned the sauce, and when I put the cabbage in the pot to boil, water spilled everywhere on the burners. I have the windows open and the fans on. The cottage should smell all right when we get back."

He laughed. "You don't have to cook for me. Ever. I just like your company."

"That's a good thing, because I'm never turning on my stove again."

"That might be safer."

She glared. "I'm starving. Drive me to town."

On the way to Ralph's, she told him that she'd been happy because she had a three-day weekend with Memorial Day. "I thought I had extra time, so I could learn to cook."

"And you picked something complicated for your first meal?"

She shrugged. "If I could make cabbage rolls, I figured I could make lots of things."

"The key word there is *if*." He winced when she punched his arm.

A family was leaving a table when they walked into the diner, and Jules motioned them to it. "Just give me a minute to clean it."

"I thought you always ate with Daphne on Saturday nights," Joel said.

"I usually do, but her parents invited her to a concert tonight, so we switched things around."

"Works for me. That way I get to see you."

She smiled. She wore only a minimum of makeup tonight—just mascara and blush. God, she was a turn-on. When Jules came for their order, she asked for her regular: a bacon cheeseburger with fries. Joel chose a fish sandwich. "I ate a big lunch. I need something a little lighter now."

They made small talk while they ate, and Miriam insisted on paying the bill. Joel wondered what would happen when he drove her home. Would she give him a quick wave when she headed for the house? But when he pulled in her drive, she said, "The smoke should be gone by now. Want a beer?"

"That sounds great." Anything that got him inside Miriam's house sounded perfect.

She led him to the backyard and went to get their drinks. He sank into one of the Adirondack chairs and stared at the ripples on the lake. What a gorgeous setting. He'd never get tired of this view. Tuppence jumped on his lap and he automatically started petting her.

Miriam returned with their beers. "You'll have to kick her off when you're sick of her or she'll never leave. She's an attention whore."

He laughed. "I guess there are worse things. It's beautiful out here. I bet you sit here every night in warm weather."

"Yup, I do. I never get tired of it." Tommy jumped onto her lap.

"How will you spend your long weekend?" he asked. "Is this your big push to get all your paperwork done?"

She shook her head. "I have more planning time next week with the seniors gone. I can coast from here."

He grinned. "It must be nice."

"It is. Why don't you come with me to my parents' house tomorrow? I don't have to leave early."

"They won't mind?"

"They liked you."

"Can I bring something?"

"It'll only be your second time. You still have a Free Pass card. Enjoy it while you can. Once your brewery's in full swing, they'll expect beer."

"Sounds fair to me."

As the sun sank lower to the horizon, Miriam stood and led him inside. She headed to the round table in the living room, and he thought she was going to offer him dessert. Instead, she said, "How about a game of Scrabble?"

Scrabble? Really? He sucked at word games, but he didn't want to leave yet. "Sure, why not?"

She showed no mercy. Miss English Teacher trounced him hard and then she gloated about it. Finally, he pulled a deck of cards out of his pocket. "Poker's my game, remember? Are you ready to lose?"

"Only if the stakes are high enough. One piece of clothing for each time I beat you."

He stared. "Aren't you worried I'll get the wrong idea? That you're easy?"

She snorted. "I am easy. With you, anyway. I don't expect any man to want to marry me, but I'd sure love to find a friend with benefits, and you fit the bill."

He didn't know what to say. "No woman's ever thought of me as a boy toy before. I'm not exactly hunk material."

"And I'm not exactly any man's dream girl, so I think we'll be a perfect fit."

Not really. He wanted more than that, but he'd ease into phase two. He didn't want to scare her off. He shuffled the cards. "Be prepared to get naked, woman."

The corners of her mouth quirked. "We'll see who loses his undies first."

He dealt a hand and had to work not to smirk. He held three kings and two queens. He glanced at Miriam, and she *did* smirk. Oh hell.

"I'm good," she told him.

"Me too. Let's see what you've got."

She laid down three aces with a gleam of triumph. He laid down his full house and she stared. "You stacked the deck."

"Quit whining. Pull that T-shirt over your head." Her skin was smooth mocha. His fingers itched to touch it. But she took the cards from him and shuffled them. She quirked an eyebrow.

"Let's see who wins this hand." She dealt and he smiled.

She picked up her cards and frowned. Hopefully, she had nothing. She looked at him. "Well?"

"I'm good," he said again.

She threw away three cards and didn't look happy with the three new ones. He only had a pair of kings, but that was enough. She took off one shoe.

"You have cute toes."

She rolled her eyes. "My feet are long and narrow. There's nothing cute about them."

"I like them. Maybe I'll lick your arches."

Her blue eyes went wide. "Are you a fetish person?"

"Nope. I just like almost everything about you."

She shook her head. "You're a sick man, but I like you."

He dealt next and got two nines and two tens. Two pairs, but lousy ones. She got three of a kind and smashed him.

"Shirt off," she said.

This was where the fun might end. He was active enough to be in tolerable shape, but he'd never had a six-pack like Tyne and Chase, and once he'd hit thirty-five, he'd had a little tummy. He knew he looked self-conscious and she grinned at him.

"I like tummies."

"You're a rare bird. You know that, right?"

"Did you want ordinary?"

"When I can have eccentric? Where's the fun in that?"

She laughed and dealt the cards. He won. The second shoe slid off. Quite a few hands later, they were each down to their undies. Hers were white and lacy and matched the bra she'd had on. His were SpongeBob boxers his mother had bought him for Christmas.

"Really?" she said when she saw them.

"A joke from my mom. I wasn't thinking fast enough. I should have worn my Star Wars pair. They're sexier."

She dealt, picked up her cards, and smirked. Damn! Did the woman always win? He picked up his cards and leveled a look her way. "Bring it on," he said.

She spread out a flush, king high. He couldn't help the look of triumph on his face. He spread out a royal flush, ace high. "Remove the panties." His voice sounded hoarse.

She stood, all six feet of smooth, supple skin, put her fingers under her lacy skimp of fabric, and wriggled out of them. His heart clutched, stopped in his chest. He took a sharp breath. When was the last time he'd seen a naked woman?

"Damn, you're beautiful."

She rolled her eyes. "You've played mommy too long."

She had a point. He got a sudden case of nerves. "What now?"

"If you don't drop your drawers and screw me, I'm going to be disappointed."

"I wouldn't want that to happen."

She motioned to a room off the hallway. "My bedroom's in there."

A king-size four-poster took up most of the room. A large walk-in closet, its door ajar, offered ample storage. The space was lovely, with wooden floors and a beamed ceiling. She tugged down the bedspread and sheets and sprawled on the mattress, raising her arms to him.

Oh God. He wanted her so much it hurt. He tossed his boxers aside and stretched himself on his side, next to her. He wanted to take it slow, to make it good for her. But she rolled over, clamped her hand around his erection, and smashed her lips against his. Okay, forget slow and gentle. He met her passion with his own. Their lips ground together, then his hands were all over her, feeling the firmness of her breasts and stomach, as hers explored him. He couldn't control himself, but neither could she. Her hand pumped up and down and he had to grab her wrist to stop her or he'd come right there and then.

She pulled him on top of her, and before he knew it, the deed was done. She smiled up at him. "I just knew you were going to be good!"

He panted to catch his breath. "You're incredible."

"*We're* incredible."

They *were* pretty damned good. After he'd married April, he'd had to buy her presents and coax her into having sex. She'd never been in the mood. With Miriam, he was lucky to keep up.

Miriam rolled onto her stomach and propped her elbow on the mattress. "Let's arm wrestle for who'll be on top next."

"You want to do it again?"

She glanced at his sagging erection. "Can you?"

"Damned if I know. April never wanted to."

She pursed her lips. "You haven't been with anyone else since you divorced?"

"I'm not too in to one-night stands and I've been busy. I was either working or at home with Adele."

She grew serious. "You're a good man."

"And you're a good woman."

She reached over and touched his face. "We won't rush this. Can you spend the night? I want to spoon against you, and I promise not to make you breakfast in the morning."

"No burned eggs?"

She punched his arm. "I make really good toast."

"Then I'll stay."

She sighed and came to snuggle against him. When they finally settled for sleep, he lay on his side and she pressed herself against his back with her arm thrown over him. He could hardly believe how good that made him feel. April had always slept as far away from him as she could get. It had made him feel alone in his own marriage. Miriam made him feel wanted. A little stab of pain pierced his chest. He didn't know how long this would last, but he was determined to enjoy every moment of it while he could.

# Chapter 19

Miriam blinked awake and knew Joel was awake, too, but he hadn't gotten out of bed. She shifted away from him to stretch and he turned to look at her.

"Good morning." He leaned forward to kiss the tip of her nose.

"How long have you been awake?"

"About half an hour, but I wasn't in any hurry to get up. I wanted to enjoy the feel of you."

Man, the guy had a way of making her feel special. "Did you sleep all right in a new bed?"

"Best sleep I've had for a while."

She grinned. "I should brush my teeth. They feel grungy. I have a spare toothbrush in the cupboard. I bought it yesterday."

"In case?" He looked amused.

"Hey, even though I lost at cards, I won. I got lucky."

"It was a win-win for both of us." He stood, and she took her time, looking him up and down.

"I'm nothing to brag about," he told her.

"That's where you're wrong. I like cozy. You look comfortable."

He laughed. "Some men wouldn't take that as a compliment."

She bit her bottom lip. "I meant it as one."

"I know, but when you play strip poker with the next guy you lure here for burned cabbage rolls, you've got to up your game, tell him how manly he looks."

She could feel her confidence leave her. "How temporary is this?"

"I'm in it for as long you'll keep me, but when you get bored with me and move on, you have to improve your come-hither chat."

She shrugged and started to the bathroom. "Screw that. If they don't measure up to you, they can take a hike."

Suddenly, he was behind her, his arms circling her waist and tugging her closer. "Do you mean that?"

"Damned straight."

He nuzzled his cheek against her back, and she thought she might die of pleasure, he made her feel so secure, so *wanted*. "I'm so glad I met you, Miriam Reinhardt. You make me happy."

She did? She rested her elbow on the bathroom countertop and raised her eyebrows at him. "Are you good at arm wrestling?"

He grinned. "Darlin', I'm handy at lots of things."

He beat her easily, then they brushed their teeth and he got to be on top. "But I'm a good sport," he told her. "We'll take turns."

She thoroughly enjoyed being in charge but couldn't decide which she liked better. Being the doer or the done to. And then she laughed at herself. She didn't have to choose. Joel didn't care either way. Her friend came with more benefits than she'd ever imagined.

They had to scramble to get showered and dressed to get to her mom's house on time. She drove, and he didn't mind that either. She got the feeling Joel didn't care if he was in the driver's seat or a passenger, as long as they were headed in the right direction. He was the most secure man she'd ever met.

When Miriam reached her parents' house, she waved at Sue-Ellen's boys, playing PIG at the basketball hoop. She grabbed Joel's hand and tugged him into the house. Her mother dropped what she was doing and hurried to give him a hug. "You're not just interested in my daughter for the free food, are you?"

She'd caught him off guard. He glanced at Miriam, and a blush crept all the way to his hairline. Mom's jaw dropped. "Oh God, the food's your last priority, isn't it? Is Miriam finally getting some nooky?"

Joel looked like he was going to die of embarrassment, and everyone turned to grin at him.

"Leave him alone," Miriam complained, "or he'll run."

Her dad shook his head. "Doesn't look like a runner to me. He has more substance than that."

Neil watched Miriam tighten her grip on Joel's hand. "He must be pretty good. Miriam's not going to let him get away."

Joel had regained his composure and laughed with the others. "No worries," he said. "I'd like to stick around a while."

Mom patted his arm. "You'll have to get used to us. We're an ill-mannered lot, but we always have one another's backs."

"I figured that."

His parents were always there for him, too, Miriam knew, but they must not be as rowdy as her family. "You guys have given him a hard enough time," she said. "How can we pitch in to get food on the table?"

Sue-Ellen grabbed a roasting pan filled with a baked spaghetti casserole. "Everything's ready. We just need to carry it to the table."

Clair grabbed the second casserole. Miriam brought one of the salads and Joel the other. Max brought a platter mounded with garlic bread and Neil scooped up the salad dressings. He stopped at the door to call for the boys. Once they'd taken their places, Dad bowed his head and said, "Please bless us and this food. Thanks for everything."

Concise but sincere. Her dad never erred on the side of flowery. Her family tended to be a bit blunt. They got to the point.

Whatever Mom had done to the spaghetti casserole was fantastic. Miriam dove in for seconds. "This is the best you've ever made it."

Mom grinned. "Same as always. I'd just say you have a bigger appetite than usual."

Damn! Maybe Mom was right. She'd probably burned a lot more calories than usual.

Joel shook his head. "I've never had it before, but it's delicious."

"Thank you." Mom's eyes twinkled, but she didn't comment.

The boys frowned. "We missed something, didn't we?"

"You're kids. You're supposed to miss things." Neil handed them the platter and they took more garlic bread.

Sam shrugged and changed the subject. "If we put up the volleyball net, will you guys play?"

"I'm in." Sue-Ellen smirked at Clair. "Maybe she won't be able to jump as high to block now."

"I don't even show." Clair patted her flat stomach. "You'd better watch the net."

At the end of the meal they all stood to clear the table and rinse the dishes. Then Dad went to the refrigerator and carried a huge bowl of tiramisu to the dining room.

Joel shook his head. "You made this yourself?"

Mom looked pleased. "It's not that hard. It just takes a little work and some planning ahead."

Joel took a taste. "I love it."

Everyone did. Every bite was gone before they headed outside. The boys kept licking the sides of the glass bowl while they rinsed the dessert dishes. Then the boys hustled outdoors to set up the volleyball net.

Miriam and Joel ended up on opposite sides. "Have you played volleyball since high school?" she asked him.

He shook his head. "I like gentler sports, like birdwatching and bowling."

She snorted. "I'm giving you fair warning: My family plays for blood."

Miriam's mother sat out, preferring to watch them from a lawn chair. Joel volunteered to sit out, too, to make the teams even, but Neil said not to worry about it. Miriam didn't think he was worried. She was pretty sure he didn't want to play but couldn't think of a graceful way out of it. She felt a little sorry for him, but it would look like she was coddling him if she gave him a pass.

Dad served the first ball, and Max hit it straight up in the air to set it up for Clair. She slammed it over the net. Toby served next and got two points for Joel's team. That annoyed Sue-Ellen, so she served to Joel, hoping he'd be his team's weak link. He set it up for Clair, though, and, as usual, Clair killed it.

By the time Miriam made it to the front row, Joel's team was ahead by five points. Unheard of. When the ball came to her, she spiked it as hard as she could. Straight into Joel's face. Within seconds his nose had swollen and his eyes were watering.

"Time out!" Mom glared at Miriam. "Really? Did you have to? Are you trying to give your boyfriend two black eyes?"

Toby's jaw dropped. "Her boyfriend?"

Sam snickered. "Don't date a girl like her. You might not survive it."

Mom grabbed Joel's arm and led him toward the house. "I'll get you some ice." She touched his nose and he winced. "I don't think she broke it, but it's going to hurt for a while."

Joel's lips set in a thin line. He looked totally embarrassed. "Go ahead without me," he told them. He wouldn't make eye contact with any of them.

Shit. Had she blown it just to score a point? Who cared if Joel was good at volleyball? What the hell had she been thinking?

"Way to go, Sis!" Sue-Ellen had to rub it in.

"I feel terrible." She knew she was competitive, but did she really need to compete with Joel? Did she always have to win?

Toby didn't help. "Yeah, the guy told you he wasn't good at volleyball."

Dad waved them to a stop. "It was an accident. We all play too hard. That's why your mom won't play with us."

Neil's shoulders drooped. "We sort of bullied him to play."

"Sort of?" Max shook his head. "You guys are ruthless. You scared the crap out of me when I first met you."

"Lesson learned," Clair said. "If someone doesn't want to play, it's no big deal."

Miriam fidgeted. "You guys go ahead without me. I'm going inside to check on Joel."

Sam made kissing sounds. "Mom always says a kiss makes things better."

"Stuff it," Miriam told him. She felt miserable. She'd hurt Joel.

The boys laughed; then Sam served the ball. Clair jumped to block it. Things were back to normal. Except for her. She was doing the walk of shame to the house, hoping Joel would forgive her.

When she entered the kitchen, her mom glared at her. "Well? What do you have to say for yourself?"

Joel was holding an ice pack to his nose.

"I'm sorry. I goaded you into playing."

He leveled a gaze on her. "Yes, you did. But never again. From now on, I sit on the sidelines with your mom whenever I want to. I don't have to prove anything to anybody. You either like me, as is, or forget it."

She blinked. She didn't think Joel had a speech like that in him. But he kept surprising her, didn't he? "I like you as is."

Her mom looked like she might faint. She put a hand to her throat, surprised.

"What now?" Miriam asked.

He handed her mom the ice pack and raised his eyebrows at her.

The swelling was already going down a little. "You drive me home and kiss it better," he said.

Her mom put a hand over her mouth to keep from laughing.

Relief rushed through her. She thought she might dance with happiness. "I can do that."

"I might need a pain pill first."

"I can do that, too." Lord, she liked this man. Really, really liked him.

"Then let's quit talking and start doing." He started to the door.

She hurried to join him.

Her family waved as they pulled down the driveway. They liked Joel, too. She wanted to pinch herself, she felt so lucky. This might be her best summer ever, if she didn't blow it before school started. She'd try to be on her best behavior. She wanted to make this last.

# Chapter 20

Monday was Memorial Day. No work. Sleeping in. The town had a parade at ten; then, for lunch, Chase and Harley were grilling hot dogs and hamburgers on the beach.

Joel woke at eight and tried not to stir. His legs were entangled with Miriam's, his arm wrapped over her torso. He nuzzled his face against her smooth skin and savored the scent of her. He never was one to lie in bed, but he meant to treasure every minute of this he could. A half hour later, when she woke, she snuggled closer to him.

"Good morning," he murmured in her ear.

"You're awake?"

"Have been. Just lying here enjoying the feel of you."

She glanced at the clock and sighed. "We'd better get ready if we're going to make it to the parade on time. Everyone will notice if we're late."

And she meant everyone. Most of the town showed up for the event.

"I need some clean clothes to wear." He lifted his arm to release her. "We'll have to stop at my apartment in town."

"I'll be quick, then." She popped out of bed and showered and put on a sundress. Her dark curls bounced around her face as they dried. He thought she looked adorable.

His shower was even faster. On the drive to town she asked, "Do I get to help you pick your outfit?"

He frowned. "You aren't one of those people who want couples to dress like each other, are you?"

"Wouldn't that be cute?" When he flinched, she laughed. "No, not my thing, but I've seen some of the outfits you put together."

"Really? I thought I did a pretty good job."

"I know. That's why I want to help you."

"We'll see."

She was driving, as usual. They parked behind Daphne's stained-glass shop and climbed the steps to his place. It looked a little lonely because both he and Adele had been away for so long. Miriam went straight to his closet and started sorting through his clothes.

"Nope. Not that one." She pulled out a pair of ripped and torn jeans. "These need to be thrown away."

"They're my work jeans."

"Doesn't matter." She finally settled on a red T-shirt and black, knee-length shorts.

"You're sort of bossy. You know that, right?" Joel put the jeans back on the rack. "I love these. They stay."

She made a face but didn't argue. When he was dressed, she looked him up and down. "You look good enough to eat, but we'd better go. We're barely going to make it in time."

They carried two folding chairs to Lake Drive. It was easier to walk than try to find a place to park. Even then, they had a hard time finding a spot to sit to watch the parade. They saw Tyne and Daphne sitting with her parents. Harley and Kathy sat with Chase and Paula. They gave them a quick wave before the Mill Pond High band started down the street, with girls tossing batons, drums pounding, and horns blasting. Behind them, Meg's hardware store had sponsored a float that she pulled behind her pickup. A painted piece of heavy plywood was painted to look like a brick street, and on each side of it, small booths were set up, with striped awnings advertising the specialty food shops in Mill Pond. Next, equestrians rode horses, and then an army of small kids from the preschool drove battery-operated cars with parents walking beside them. Antique tractors rumbled down the street next, and finally, the parade ended with two more floats: the Boy Scouts crowded on one with tents set up on the far end and Ian's resort featured the other with a beautiful fake garden filled with potted flowers.

Joel had seen better parades, but he knew almost every participant in this one, which made it special. Once the parade was over, people milled around, visiting with one another. Miriam's family came to greet them and then drifted off to chat with friends. Joel pumped more hands than he ever had, but that was what he liked about Mill Pond. Most people were friendly.

At noon Chase and Harley took their places behind four grills, and soon, they were passing out burgers and dogs. Paula and Tyne had made big batches of baked beans and potato salad. Art had donated bags of chips. It was a low-key event, and people ate, then wandered off to yak with clusters of friends, walk the beach, and watch kids play in the shallow water of the lake.

Miriam saw Maya with Paula's mother, Hazel, and made a bee-line for them. "Maya, this is Joel. And Joel, this is Maya and Paula's mom, Hazel." She smiled at the girl. "Are you enjoying your summer break?"

Maya glanced at Hazel and the woman gave her a firm nod. Uh-oh[ something was up. Miriam noticed, too, and frowned.

"Go ahead. Tell her," Hazel said.

Maya firmed her shoulders and looked up, past them, then gave a big smile. Joel turned to see a kid with scruffy hair and whiskers walking toward them. When Miriam saw him, her lips tightened into a thin line.

Joel gently touched Miriam's arm. "This must be T. J." He held out his hand to greet the boy.

Miriam looked surprised but waited to see what would happen.

T. J. moved to stand beside Maya. He was a good-looking boy. Joel could see why girls fell for him, but he was smarter than Miriam gave him credit for. His gray eyes sparkled with intelligence. Right now, he wore a fierce scowl. He reached for Joel's hand and pierced him with a quick scrutiny.

"If you let us explain, it's not as bad as Miss Reinhardt thinks."

Joel nodded, encouraging him.

T. J. wrapped his arm through Maya's. "I was never very good at schoolwork, but I'm not stupid. I just didn't like it."

Miriam nodded agreement. "You're plenty smart. I never questioned that."

T. J.'s shoulders relaxed a little. "I'm starting at a trade school soon, getting paid while I'm learning furnace and air conditioning. I won't make good money for two years, but I'll make enough to rent a house and pay our bills." He looked at Maya. "I want to be with her. She can drive back and forth to Bloomington for her classes. I love how smart she is. I love how strong she is."

Joel studied him. "You're both really young. I got married young, and it was a mistake."

T. J. shrugged. "My parents got married right out of high school and they're still together. Still happy."

Hazel cast her vote with T. J. "I married my Pete right out of high school, just before he joined the military. I never regretted it."

"Are you ready to settle down?" Miriam frowned at T. J., unconvinced.

Maya answered this time. "Neither of us wants to get married or to spend every second with each other. If he sees his friends a couple times a week, I don't care. Then I can do what I want to. But he'd better always make me feel like I come first."

T. J. grinned. "If she's unhappy, she lets me know. I like that about her. I'm the one who'd like to get married. It scares me that she'll meet someone smart and cool in college and I won't be good enough for her."

Maya gave an exasperated sigh. "That's not going to happen."

"It could," T. J. argued. "But I'm going to make you so happy, you won't want anyone else."

Miriam blinked and Joel smiled. She hadn't thought about this scenario. The mousy little girl she'd told him about wasn't as mousy as she looked. Joel guessed the girl had an inner core of steel. "I think they have a shot."

"So do I." Miriam hesitated. She still had doubts but was willing to concede.

Maya let out a breath of relief. "Thank you. I know this isn't what you wanted."

"When is life ever that easy?" Miriam tossed up her hands in defeat.

Hazel glanced at Paula and Chase and her two grandkids on the beach. "Nothing goes according to plan. Sometimes it turns out even better than expected."

T. J. tugged at Maya. "You feel better now?"

The girl blushed and nodded at Miriam. "I didn't want to tell you. I didn't want you to be disappointed in me."

"Hey, a girl's got to do what a girl's got to do." Miriam waved them away. "Go have fun. I wish you the best."

Joel watched Hazel, Maya, and T. J. head to the beach to join Paula and Chase. He raised his eyebrows at Miriam. "Are you really okay?"

"Yeah, but I need a little pick-me-up. Tommy and Tuppence will miss you if you don't come home with me. Want to come to my place for supper?"

*Uh-oh.* "You're not going to cook, are you?"

"Nope, but there's a meal waiting for us."

He knew this woman and her appetites. "I'll need more than a tuna salad sandwich."

She gave a secretive smile. "It's a surprise."

That worried him, but when they got back to her cottage, Daphne and Tyne were already there. The water was still cool, but they were swimming. They came to shore when they saw them. Wonderful aromas drifted from the kitchen and Joel felt himself drool. "What did you make this time?" It was hard not to stare at Tyne's eight-pack abs. How did the man cook all day and still look like that? It wasn't fair.

Tyne grinned. "I decided to keep it simple. I made a sheet-pan meal of chicken quarters, potatoes, and carrots. It's in the oven, cooked, and all I have to do is reheat it later."

Joel had no idea what a sheet-pan meal was, but it smelled wonderful. Garlic and onions permeated the kitchen. He heaved a sigh of relief and Miriam raised an eyebrow.

"I heard that."

He didn't deny it. "Can you boil an egg?"

She pursed her lips, hesitant to answer. Finally, she said, "No."

"My point exactly."

Tyne laughed. "Everyone's good at different things. Miriam said you'd help me put out the pier. She lets us use her pontoon, but I'd like to buy a boat this year to keep at the marina. I want to teach Daphne to tube."

Daphne stared at him, alarmed. "You didn't tell me that."

"You'll love it."

Joel decided that was between them and headed to the shore with Tyne to help with the pier. A neighbor came by to lend a hand and Tyne invited him to supper. "There's plenty."

And there was. Tyne didn't cook small portions. Three hours later they all stopped for supper, which was delicious, as always when Tyne made it, then went back to work. In an another hour the pier was ready to go, and Joel drove Tyne to the marina to claim Miriam's pontoon. Then they loaded the girls onboard for a short ride before the sun set.

When they returned to the cottage, Tyne stretched and sighed. "I love the water. It relaxes me."

"Me too. It makes me tired." Daphne reached for his hand and tugged him toward her yellow SUV. "It's back to work tomorrow, but this was fun. Thanks."

"Thanks for the supper, and borrow the pontoon any time."

When they left, shadows stretched across the lawn and stars twinkled into view. Miriam nodded toward the house.

Joel shook his head. "Don't expect much tonight. It's been a long day."

"I'll be gentle."

Like hell she would. But the bed felt wonderful and he loved the room itself—her four-poster bed, the beams on the ceiling, and the deep window casings. She tugged his T-shirt over his head and he thought of Tyne. No firm abs here, but Miriam didn't seem to care. He couldn't believe how lusty she was, but it suited her personality. She didn't shy away from anything. Once they sank onto the bed, he said, "Remember. Be docile."

She snorted. "Right."

Wrong word choice. But it didn't matter. Miriam always excited him. Once they'd finished, though, and rolled to spoon each other, they both fell asleep.

# Chapter 21

Miriam didn't want to get up when the alarm buzzed. Only four more days of school and she was almost as unmotivated as her students. Not that she could have Joel all to herself today anyway. His alarm buzzed, too, and he had to rush into town to shower and get dressed for work. He yanked on his clothes and bent to kiss her good-bye.

"Damn it." She sat up, scooting the cats to the foot of the bed. Tuppence took it in her stride. Tommy glared and moved begrudgingly. "I wish I could tie you to the bedpost and have my way with you."

He mussed her curls. "No need to. You can have your way with me whenever you want to."

"Tonight?" She held her breath, waiting for his answer.

"Perfect, I'll pick up something to eat on my way here."

"You just don't want me to cook."

"There's that, too."

She threw herself back on the mattress. The cats stared at her in surprise. Since when had she gotten so melodramatic? But the days were going too fast. Soon, Adele would be home again, and then what would happen? Would he kick her to the curb? Spend all his time with his daughter? That was one of the things she admired about him, that he was a devoted dad. And once he opened the brewery, he'd be even busier. Would he make time for her? Ever?

He laughed at her exaggerated suffering. "I take it something's bothering you?"

"I'm going to miss you when Adele gets back, and it's going to be even worse when you open the brewery. You won't have time for me."

He studied her. "That depends."

She sat up again, intrigued. "On what?"

"On where Adele and I live. If we moved in with you, you'd get sick of seeing us. We'd be underfoot when you were ready to call it a day and relax."

Move in with her? Was he serious? The last time she'd had a roommate was in college. But if he stayed in his apartment and worked long hours at the brewery, she'd only get bits and pieces of his time, and eventually, he'd even get tired of that.

He shook his head. "We'll figure something out. I'll *make* time for you."

She watched him walk away, and somehow, it felt symbolic. Final. Yes, he was coming back tonight and, hopefully, the night after that and the night after that. But it wasn't enough. She wanted him. She wanted to wake up to him every morning and to fall asleep with him every night. But did she want forever? How long would this feeling last? She had no idea, but she was pretty sure she'd feel empty and hollow without him. Could they just play house for a while and see where that led?

What about Adele? If they moved in together and it didn't work, would she feel abandoned when Joel moved into his own house?

# Chapter 22

Joel made two stops on his way to Miriam's that night. One was at Art's Grocery. The other was for a surprise for Miriam. When he pulled into her drive, he saw her and her cats, sitting in the backyard, staring at the lake. A book lay open on her lap. He grabbed the bag of groceries and went to join her.

"Do you have a grill?" He hadn't paid as much attention as he should have. Lately, his mind was on other things.

She stood to give him a kiss, to nuzzle against him. He loved the feel of her. She motioned to the gas grill near the kitchen door at the edge of the patio.

He grinned. "I bought salmon steaks on cedar planks."

She frowned when he showed them to her. "They're on wood. Won't they burn?"

"Oh, woman, you have no cooking finesse at all." He pulled out half a dozen zucchini. "These are great on the grill, too."

"If you say so."

Her eyes lit up when he showed her a tub of pasta salad. *Pitiful.* "I should have known. The one you recognize is premade."

She had no shame and went to get them each a beer. She hovered around while he grilled the food, carrying plates and silverware to the circular picnic table when supper was ready. They ate with a soft breeze blowing across the lake, the air soft against his skin. She told him about her day.

"I'll have all my paperwork finished by Thursday. We only have a half day of school on Friday and that's a goof-off day. Some of the faculty challenge the basketball team to a silly twenty-point game in the auditorium. Then kids are allowed to yak and get their yearbooks signed before they leave."

"Sounds like a nice way to end the year."

"It is." She carried the dirty dishes into the kitchen and came back with two more beers. They went to sit in the Adirondack chairs. They'd pulled them closer to each other, so their legs touched. She glanced at him sideways. "You go to pick up Adele on Saturday, don't you?"

He surprised her by saying, "Want to come along?"

She'd been trying to steer the conversation to him and Adele, but this threw her off. "To spend a day with your parents?" That sounded scary. She fidgeted nervously.

"They like you."

"For real?" She'd worried about that. Daphne's parents had always treated her like a bother, giving the impression they'd be happy if Daphne became immune to her.

"I've met your family." He took another sip of his beer.

Her family could be intimidating, but he'd braved them anyway. Fair was fair. "Then, yeah, why not?"

A small smile lifted his lips. "If they're polite to you, they don't like you. If they give you grief, you're in."

She laughed. The same could be said of her folks. A duck swam past them, slowing down to scope for food. Miriam shooed him away. "I've seen your messy ways. No handouts here."

Tommy ran toward the water, crouching to spring—not that he would. He hated to get wet. The duck didn't know that and left.

"Did you train him to do that?" Joel asked.

"Nope, but I like it." She scooped up the cat when he sauntered back toward them and settled him on her lap.

Not to be left out, Tuppence jumped on Joel and curled up. He stroked her smooth fur and gave a satisfied sigh. "I'm hoping to have the restaurant finished on Friday."

She blinked at him, surprised. "Then what? Are you doing a grand opening?"

"I've hired enough staff, but I have to admit, I'm a little nervous. I wish I had a backup manager for a few weeks, just to see how things go."

"When do you open?"

"Next Monday. The beer's ready. The tanks are full. The food supplies are in, and Tyne went over them with me to make sure I had enough. I've researched everything out the kazoo and bantered ideas around with Ian, Chase, and Harley, but I'm still worried I forgot something."

"Hey, who wouldn't get a case of nerves before their grand opening? I'll show up next week every day if you need me. I can't cook, but I'm great at dishing up."

He stared. "You'd really do that? Just to help me out?"

"We're friends. No, we're more than that." Something in his expression tugged at her heart. Hadn't anyone ever come through for this man but his parents? "I don't have to wear roller skates, do I?"

That caught him off guard. He tossed back his head and laughed. "No, but I'd love to see that."

"Won't happen."

They finished their beers and finally headed inside. He stopped at the door and said, "Forgot. I have something in the truck." When he returned, he carried a froufrou little bag with lots of tissue paper inside. He handed it to her.

She took it, her brows furrowed in suspicion. "This doesn't look like chocolate."

"Does everything revolve around food for you?"

"Not everything."

"Look inside."

She pulled out a black, sexy, push-up bra and a thong. Her eyes went wide. "Good God, I don't have anything to push up. I'm skin and bones—tall and gawky. I'll look like Olive Oyl in these."

He shook his head. "Hey, your boobs are perky. There's a good cupful each. Anyway, Popeye thought Olive Oyl was sexy, so it's all in the eye of the beholder."

That was the beauty of him. He really *did* think she was sexy. He made her feel special. "Let's go see how they fit."

He smiled. "*That's* what I was looking forward to."

# Chapter 23

Joel spent every night at Miriam's house for the rest of the week. She'd never said a thing about when Adele came home, so he assumed they'd go back to the way things were—with him staying in his apartment and them seeing each other occasionally—but he was determined to see her as often as he could. True, she'd volunteered to help out when the brewery opened next week, but they'd be so busy, they'd hardly have time to talk. He'd toyed with the idea of closing on Sundays, like Chase did, so that he'd have one day off a week. Most shops in Mill Pond closed then, but boy, if he stayed open, he'd have lots of business, so he'd decided to put in the time and go for the extra income. He couldn't spend all day, every day there, though, so he hired an assistant to share the hours—a kid taking business classes at IU, home on summer break.

"I'll work as many hours as you give me," Collin said. "I need the money."

They'd decided to work most of the week together to get a feel for things, then Collin would take over Sundays and three evenings on his own. But first, Joel needed to finish the final details of the brewery. The kitchen appliances were in, but the fixtures needed to be installed. The furniture needed to be arranged, but they could easily wrap up everything before the weekend.

By two on Friday afternoon everything was officially finished and ready for business, and Joel loved the way things had turned out. Bright colors. Great floor plan. And great food and beers. Tyne had come over one afternoon and they'd made every offering on the menu to test them out. Once Tyne gave him the nod of approval, he felt pretty damn good.

"I'd give you five stars," Tyne said.

A chef's approval? That was enough for Joel.

Chase and Ian had come to test the beers. The tanks were at full volume now, and Joel would offer five varieties when he opened.

"*Mmm*, I like the Big M lager." Chase smirked. "You must have been feeling pretty inspired. And the Sweet Blonde ale is a close second. If you have enough to supply my bar, I'll put in an order for both."

Ian drained his sample of Mill Pond IPA and poured himself a mug. "I want this one for the resort. It has great balance."

They'd already talked numbers—volume and prices—so Joel nodded and said, "Can do. The last two?"

"They're great," Chase said, "but too serious for my customers. People who are really in to beer are going to love them, though. They're going to be sellers here."

That's what Joel had thought, too. His food had passed Tyne's critique and his beers had passed Chase and Ian, so he was feeling pretty good. Everything looked like it was ready to go.

When the last fixture had been hung and the last detail dealt with, Nick stalled a little, almost sad to walk out the brewery's door for the last time. "I'm going to miss coming here. You've been great to work for."

Joel handed him a stack of envelopes, one for each man on the crew. "Then come back and have a few free meals on me."

"Really? Thanks, man. Will do."

"The doors open on Monday. What's your next job?"

Nick put his last tool in his toolbox. "We're working with my dad and brother on a big project two towns over. It'll be back to lunch boxes for sure. And I finished my flip house in Indy. It's already sold, so I bought a new fixer-upper in town."

"In Mill Pond?" That surprised Joel. "Does that mean Roxy's out of the picture?"

"Yup, I've moved on. I'm going to stick close to town for a while. Grabbed one of the places Iris Clinger's been showing for a couple of months. The owner dropped the price enough that I can make a decent profit."

"Which one?" Joel had looked at every available house in the entire area.

"The trilevel on the far side of the lake."

Joel gave a low whistle. "I went through that one and decided it would take too much work." The aluminum siding was faded. The carpets should have died a few years ago. The rooms were small and choppy.

"Exactly." Nick grinned. "That's why no one else wanted it either. Those are the perfect ones for me."

Joel could see that. "Well, the brewery isn't that far from the lake. We're open on weekends. You could stop by for lunch sometime."

Nick rubbed his chin. "You know, Meg helped me look at that house, check the plumbing. It's in bad shape. I can do all the work, but I needed to know if I could get everything locally. That girl knows her stuff, gave me a few ideas, so I owe her a lunch. Maybe I'll bring her with me some Saturday."

"I like Meg. If you bring her, she can eat on the house, too." Maybe Nick would wake up and look at her as a woman, not a tag-along sister. He decided to give a small push in that direction. "I'm surprised no one's snatched her up by now. She's sure a pretty girl."

Nick blinked, surprised. "She's just a kid."

"She doesn't look like a kid to me. What is she? Early twenties?"

Nick frowned. "She's five years younger than Maddie, so that must make her . . . twenty-three?"

"Of legal age and a knockout. Somebody has to be sniffing around, trying to catch her attention."

Nick scowled. He didn't look happy about that. "Yeah, well, I'd better get going. Good luck with everything and I'll see you soon." He grabbed his tools and walked out the door for the last time as Joel's contractor.

Alone, Joel turned in a slow circle, inspecting the finished product. His brewery. Pride swelled inside him. He wanted to share this moment with someone. Miriam only taught half a day today and was probably home by now. He decided to ask her out for a special supper. They could come here, so he could show her the place before it opened, and then they could celebrate. It would be their last night together.

He made the call. "I thought I'd give you a tour of the brewery, and then we could drive to Bloomington for dinner."

"Bloomington? You're going all-out."

"Tyne told me about this great restaurant with a wood-fire oven."

"The Malibu Grill. I love it."

*Perfect.* "I'm celebrating. The brewery's ready for business. Do we have a date?"

"You had me at free food."

He laughed. His girl was pretty predictable. "I'll see you in an hour." He decided to dress for the occasion and stopped at the apartment to shower and change into Dockers and a button-down shirt. When he picked her up, she was dressed in Dockers, too, and a clingy black tee. Her boobs were higher than usual: her push-up bra.

He whistled. "You look nice."

"So do you." She sniffed him. "You're even wearing cologne." She came close to inhale him. "Sharp and spicy. I like it."

He wrapped his arms around her and pulled her to him. She ground her lips against his, ran her tongue over them, and then pulled away. "Did you make reservations?"

He nodded, out of breath. She did that to him, made him stand at attention before he could control himself.

"What time do we have to be there?"

"Six."

"Shit, we have to be good. This has to wait."

He took a deep breath, then released her reluctantly and led her to his truck. "Ready to see the brewery?"

"I can't wait."

The weather had turned warm and sticky once June hit, so he rolled up the windows and flipped on the air conditioner. No use melting on their drive across town. When he led her inside, she clapped her hands together and twirled in a happy circle, trying to take in everything at once. "It's even better than I pictured it!"

The bar had a modern, funky look, and the family room had plenty of punches of color. He'd decided on white dishes with a bright dot of color in their centers.

"The colors on the plates match your walls." Miriam looked at the tall, simple beer glasses. "This place is great."

After she'd looked at every room, he led her back outside. A double-wide trailer sat in front of the trees in the distance.

"I didn't notice that when we drove up. Is it move-in ready?"

"Yup, I even bought furniture for it."

She sounded worried when she asked, "Do you plan to move there until you find a house?"

Did that bother her? Why would it? Why would she care where he and Adele lived? He'd thrown out an offer to her and she hadn't responded, but she was doing her nervous fidget.

She shook her head. "Am I like T. J.?"

"What?" He had no idea what she was talking about.

"He loved being with Maya but didn't want a commitment until Maya left him."

Joel glanced at the trailer. He had thought about moving in for a while. There'd be more space and he'd be right by his business. If Miles needed help, he could rent a place for him. "If you're not ready to commit, you're not. You told me up-front you only wanted a friend with benefits."

She bit her bottom lip. "If you leave me, will you come back?"

He didn't see him ever leaving her. He'd rather have a short time with her than a long time with anyone else, but life didn't come with guarantees. He'd learned that the hard way. "How can I answer that? There's no way to know." She sighed, and he took her arm to lead her outside. He opened the door of his pickup and helped her climb in. "Tonight's supposed to be fun. It's to celebrate, remember? Let's go check out this Malibu Grill."

The drive took half an hour. The air had cooled a little, so they rolled down their windows, enjoying the warm June air. They didn't talk much. Miriam seemed lost in her own thoughts. When they reached Bloomington, he parked in the center of town, then looked around, confused. "It's pretty dead for a Friday night." Then he slapped his forehead. "The kids have all gone home for the summer, haven't they? College is out of session."

Miriam nodded. "Things are always slower here in the summer."

A good thing. The restaurant was busy enough that Joel was glad he'd reserved a table. A waiter led them to a four-top and asked, "Would you care for something to drink?"

Miriam ordered a beer, so he did, too

He glanced down the menu, but Miriam didn't open hers. She'd said she loved to come here. She must have a favorite.

When the waiter brought their drinks, they ordered their food.

"A bacon cheeseburger and fries for me," Miriam said.

The woman was obsessed. Joel got a kick out of that. She had no pretense, never put on airs. He ordered the Hawaiian rib eye and a baked potato.

The food was delicious. Someone played the piano in the other room. They made small talk, nothing serious, and had a wonderful night. Then, before Joel realized it, it was time to drive home.

The temperature was cooler, so they rolled down their windows. Farmers had been working in their fields and the scent of freshly turned earth hung in the air. When they got closer to Mill Pond, Miriam started to squirm. Joel knew the signs. She was getting ready to ask him something and didn't know how he'd answer. She cleared her throat. "This has been really nice. A special night. Want to come to my place to relax?"

He knew what *relax* meant and smiled. "I brought a bottle of wine and an extra set of clothes so we can get up tomorrow and leave to get Adele."

She relaxed again and smiled. Then her fingers started to fidget. "You know, I was thinking, because it's summer and everything and Adele loves the lake, my place has two bedrooms. Maybe Adele could have her own room, and you guys could spend the weekends with me."

*The weekends*. Not exactly what he'd had in mind, but it was a start. Joel stayed noncommittal. No point in moving too fast and spooking her. "She'd like that. What are you thinking about? Fridays and Saturdays?"

"That would be fun, don't you think?"

"Perfect." He'd learned patience from dealing with Adele. It was going to come in handy, dealing with Miriam, too. "We won't start tomorrow night, though. I'll let Adele settle in before everything gets busy at the brewery. She's had a week of fun, and she'll get all excited about spending the night with you. Sometimes, when she has too much stimuli, she has seizures. She takes medicine, but I'm careful about not overdoing it with her."

"Seizures?" Miriam sounded wary. Why wouldn't she?

"They're not as bad as they used to be. We've gotten a better handle on them now."

Her nervous fidgets started again. Maybe he'd frightened her away. He was so used to working with Adele, he took her issues for granted and forgot to mention them.

When they got back to her cottage, they carried a last beer outside to sit and look at the lake. A half-moon sent silver webs over the water. Stars twinkled overhead. The water lapped against the cement seawall. It was magical, soothing Joel's soul. Miriam relaxed in the chair next to him. Finally, they wandered into the house and headed to the bedroom. Their lovemaking started slow and tender. He grazed her neck, her breasts, and abdomen with his lips, gently brushed them over her inner thighs while his fingers teased her nipples. Miriam moaned, raised her hips off the bed, and dug her fingers into his back, a little needy. He rolled her over and sprinkled kisses up and down her spine, playfully nipped her firm ass, and slid his fingers between her folds, stroking gently at first. When his fingers slid inside her, she came violently and tried to push his hand away. He rolled her onto her back and entered her. She gasped when he increased his rhythm and timed his finish with hers. Then he slathered her with kisses again, doing his best to make her feel loved. Finally, they spooned together and fell asleep.

# Chapter 24

Miriam thought she'd hate being a passenger. She preferred being in charge, but Joel informed her that he'd invited her to his parents' house, so he was driving. At first she braked instinctively when she thought he should have sooner. She pointed out when a car was coming faster than usual at an intersection. And then she let herself relax. Joel was a good driver. She was better, but he was safe enough. She sat back and enjoyed the scenery.

Occasionally, she'd glance at Joel. She liked his profile. He had a strong chin, a straight nose—not too wide. His mouth was generous and seemed to half-smile perpetually.

They had a long ride and she'd been curious, so she asked, "Would you tell me about your ex-wife? Or would you rather not talk about her?"

He shrugged. "Not much to tell. We met in high school. She was really pretty, with a fragile, sad air about her. She looked like she needed rescuing, and I thought I was the guy who could do it. My brother, Miles, fights demons, but April nurtures them, encourages them. She *likes* being needy. I didn't get that for a long time. And then I knew I was doomed. April didn't want to be saved. She wanted someone to support her, to take care of all her needs, so she wouldn't have to change. We might still have made it, but April treated Adele like she was competition. She resented it when I spent time with our daughter. It finally got ridiculous and I walked."

"What does April do now?"

"She lives with a guy on disability. They have enough to keep their heads above water, but when the shit hits the fan, she calls me for help."

"And you still rush in to rescue her?"

"We have boundaries. She knows what they are and so do I."

Miriam stared at him. He was such a generous man but not a pushover. He'd found a balance in his life.

When they got close to Fort Wayne, he said, "My parents live on the south side of the city. That makes it easier." He turned off the interstate and drove to a small addition. They passed a pool, and he smiled. "Miles and I belonged to that when we were kids. Joined the swim team."

"Were you good?"

"I was okay, won a few ribbons. Never went on to the Olympics." He sounded fine with that.

"Where did you go to college?"

He gave her a look. "I didn't. I got married right out of high school and seven months later April had Adele. She'd told me she was on birth control. She wasn't. When the doctor explained about cerebral palsy, I knew my whole life had changed."

"I'm so sorry." Miriam reached out to put her hand on his thigh. "You were so young."

"I grew up fast. I worked construction and made good money, enough to invest when strip malls went up for sale, and I read a lot, but some people with degrees still look down their noses at me."

She didn't know what to say. Finally, she tried, "Sorry. I didn't mean to sound like a snob."

"I've never thought of you as one. You've never talked down to me."

"But you think I looked down on T. J. because he wasn't going to college, don't you?"

He grinned. "Nope. I think your whole focus is Maya. You see potential in that girl and want her to achieve her dreams. You can be pretty ferocious when you're trying to protect someone."

That made her feel better. She pulled her hand back and relaxed again.

He turned a corner and more neat houses with well-kept yards lined the street. He reached a modest, ranch-style house with white stonework framing its front door and pulled into the driveway. "We're here."

The door flew open and his mother came to greet them. "Miriam, we're so glad you decided to come with Joel. It's nice to see you again."

She led them inside and Adele grinned up at them from a big, dark-blue recliner that made her look small. "Dad, I had a wonderful time! Uncle Russell has so many cats, I couldn't count them all. Some let me pet them and some ran away. I even got to pet a cow!"

"A cow?" Joel ruffled her blond hair. "Do you want to be a farmer now?"

Adele shook her head. "I like Mill Pond."

Joel's mom waved them toward the long, matching sofa. "Sit down. Relax. Want something to drink?"

His dad winked at Miriam. "We have beer."

The wink made her feel at home. "I'm in."

"Me too." Joel inhaled the aromas coming from the kitchen. "Whatever you're cooking, it smells good."

His mom cocked her head. "You know what that is."

"Brisket?"

She nodded. "One of your favorites."

"I love you, Mom." He blew her a kiss, then turned to Miriam. "We used to tease Mom that she must be Jewish, she made such good briskets."

Why hadn't he mentioned that earlier? She'd have had a better chance with a slab of meat than the cabbage rolls she'd tried to make and failed.

His mom went on. "The weather's so nice, I thought we could eat on the back patio and have sort of a picnic. Does that sound okay? You must be getting hungry after your long drive."

Joel stretched his legs in front of him. "We can talk for a few minutes to relax first. Do you need any help in the kitchen?"

His dad delivered their beers and sent Miriam a wicked grin. "We heard rumors to keep a certain lady away from a stove."

Her jaw dropped. "Joel ratted me out?"

"We're his parents. He tells us everything."

She shot Joel a look and he shook his head.

"Not all." And he looked absolutely naughty.

She threw back her head and laughed. They were giving her a rough time. Joel said that meant they liked her. "I'm not much of a cook. I can make microwave popcorn, though."

"Me too!" Adele looked proud of herself and Joel's mom glanced at her affectionately.

"Our girl here is pretty talented. We sure enjoyed having her on our trip."

Joel's dad changed the subject. "So, how's the brewery coming? Is it ready to go?"

The conversation turned to how many tanks Joel had, then to how many people he could seat, and on and on. Finally, Joel's mom interrupted. She turned to Miriam. "What about you, hon? How do you spend your summers when you don't have to teach?"

"I love to read and garden."

That's all she had to say and his mom jumped up, grabbed Miriam's hand, and tugged her toward the back door. "You have to see my flowerbeds." She glanced at Adele, but the girl shook her head. She was happy cozying up in her big chair.

They left the men in the house, talking business, and she led Miriam to the backyard. They went from one bed to another. Each was immaculate, with every group of flowers neatly mulched. Miriam's beds were well-tended but a bit unruly, one set of plants bumping into another. Miriam stopped and took a deep breath when they reached his mom's irises.

"I've never seen orange ones like those." They were stunning. A brilliant, bright orange, and she lusted after them.

His mom gave a satisfied smile. "We drove to a nursery near Churubusco to buy them. Once I saw them, I had to have them. They've multiplied a lot since then. If you come with Joel in the fall, I'll dig up a few starts for you."

Miriam's hand went to her throat. What a kind offer! "You would? Are you sure?"

"For you, hon, of course I would."

Miriam reached out and hugged her but jerked away when she saw her raise a hand to dab at a tear. "Oh, I'm sorry. You don't know me that well. I didn't mean . . ."

His mom shook her head. "It's not like that. April would hardly even talk to me. She'd never touch me. I always wanted . . ." She stopped and pressed her lips in a firm line, then took a deep breath. "I'm so glad you're a hugger."

At that, Miriam crushed her in a tight embrace. She felt for this woman. "Joel's so lucky he has you two. You remind me of my parents. You're going to have to come to Mill Pond to meet my family sometime."

His mom gave a happy sigh, then pulled away to regain her composure. "You've been wonderful for Joel. He needs someone who laughs, who enjoys life."

"I laugh too loud." Miriam shrugged. "There are worse sins, right?"

"I'd rather hear someone laugh than sit there like a stick." His mom grimaced. "Sorry. I don't know where my manners have gone." She motioned toward the house. "Walt's going to want food soon. That man's stomach came with a timer. Are you ready to eat?"

"Joel says I'm always hungry. I'll help you carry stuff out."

His mom looked stunned and shook her head.

Miriam misunderstood. "I want to help."

"I'm not going to get all weepy again, but April never lifted a finger. She came here and expected to be waited on."

Miriam barked a laugh. "My family gets together every Sunday, and if you slack on pitching in, God help you."

"I like that." His mom nodded approval. "But it's going to take me a minute to get used to it." She smiled and slipped her arm through Miriam's. "You're a breath of fresh air."

Adele came to join them in the kitchen, and the two women teased her until they had her laughing. Joel and his dad came to pitch in, and before long, the patio table was covered with food—sliced brisket, spoonbread, green beans with onions and bacon, and a fruit salad.

Joel's dad talked about the car he was working on—an ongoing project—and his mom told them tidbits from their trip, with Adele chiming in. Miriam sat back and let them talk, a feeling of belonging sweeping over her. It went so deep and felt so good, it surprised her. Her family was so warm, so wonderful, she'd never felt lacking. She'd never considered the fact that *two* families might be better than one. Actually, she'd heard so many horror stories about in-laws that she'd considered them a hurdle rather than a blessing. But she was wrong. These people made her feel accepted, loved.

They lingered over their meal, then helped with cleanup and stayed a while longer, until Joel finally said, "Thanks for everything. It was great seeing you. I love you guys, and thanks for giving Adele such a good time, but we have a long ride home. We'd better get going."

They walked out the front door on their way to his pickup, everyone feeling happy and satisfied, and his parents were giving them good-bye hugs when a man with Joel's light-brown hair and gray eyes pulled a car to the curb and parked. He got out and paused when he saw Joel. Then he squared his shoulders and walked up the drive.

"Hey, Bro!"

His walk was a little unsteady and he carried a bottle wrapped in a brown paper bag.

Joel's voice was tight when he said, "Miles, meet my friend, Miriam. Miriam, my brother, Miles."

Miriam glanced at Joel's mother. Her expression said it all. Miles had fallen off the wagon again and she was crushed.

"Hey, Mom and Dad!"

Joel's dad put on a grin. He reached out a hand to his son. "Hey, kid, come on in the house. Your brother's about to leave. We have lots of leftovers. You hungry?" He wrapped an arm around Miles to keep him steady and led him inside.

"Mom?" Joel hesitated, not sure what to do.

She smiled. "We've had a wonderful visit. Let's not ruin it now. We'll deal with this. You guys head on home."

Her voice held a note of steel, and Miriam realized how strong the woman was.

Joel nodded. He understood. "If you need me, call. I'll come."

"I know that." She hugged him. "Now get out of here. We loved seeing you." And she turned to walk to the house.

The ride home wasn't as ebullient as it should have been. Joel was lost in thought. So was Miriam. And Adele, bless her, spent most of the time in her own little world.

# Chapter 25

Joel dropped off Miriam at her cottage, then headed to his apartment in town. Adele had had enough stimulation for a while. A nice, quiet night would be good for her.

Before Miriam got out, she asked, "Do you and Adele want to come to my parents' house for our Sunday get-together?"

He knew she expected a yes, but he shook his head. "Not this time. I want to take it easy before opening day on Monday." Everything had been rushed lately. He wanted to settle in to focus. Next week was going to be stressful. He and Miriam could cuddle again next Friday and Saturday . . . after he'd survived opening week.

She forced a smile. "No problem. I'll see you Monday."

It was awkward. For the first time, he felt weird around her. "I appreciate your volunteering to help. Thanks!" When he pulled away, it felt odd, leaving her place.

Back at their apartment, Adele went straight to her chair in the sitting room and turned on the TV. He let her watch the last half hour of an old movie on the Hallmark Channel while he unpacked her clothes and tossed them in the laundry basket. While he sorted through colors, he thought about Miles.

It was a Saturday, so his brother hadn't had to work. Did he let himself drink on the weekends? Did he stay sober during the week? Joel had played with the idea of moving into the trailer until he found a house for him and Adele, but he decided against that now. If Miles drank on a Friday night and Saturday, soon he'd be drinking in his evenings after work. Eventually, he wouldn't wake up for work. It was only a matter of time before he got fired and ran out of money. Then he'd have to move back in with their parents.

Joel didn't want that.

He started a load of darks and went to check on Adele. "Are you hungry?"

She shook her head. Neither was he. He'd eaten too much of his mom's home cooking. "I have an idea. What if I make popcorn and ice cream sodas and we watch a movie together? It has to be something I like, too."

"*The Little Mermaid*?"

"One of my favorites." Not really. He'd watched it with her a hundred times but didn't mind. It always made her happy. When the movie ended, she was getting tired but wasn't ready to go to sleep yet, so they watched a TV show about people who bought little houses. Some of them were on wheels and could be moved. He'd feel claustrophobic in such a cramped space, but Adele gave a happy sigh and turned to him.

"I wish I could have my own little house and be a grown-up like other kids."

"And leave me? What would I do without my sunshine?" But her words made him sad. She wasn't like other kids. Never would be.

In bed that night, his thoughts drifted to Miriam. Maybe he wanted too much. What woman would want to marry him and take on Adele? It was asking too much. Miriam's idea of friends with benefits was a lot more realistic.

Before he'd moved to Mill Pond, some friends who'd known him a long time had told him that he should consider putting Adele in a group home. "She'd be surrounded by other people, taken care of, and you could have a life."

He knew what caring for Adele cost him. He looked at the empty pillow on the other side of his bed. But he'd shaken his head. "I can't do it."

"Listen, Joel, maybe it would be the best thing for her. You wouldn't be abandoning her. You could visit her every day. And you need to think long term. What's going to happen to her when you can't take care of her anymore?"

His biggest fear. What would happen to Adele when he died? He'd have to come to terms with that someday but not now. Not yet.

# Chapter 26

Miriam dragged herself out of bed on Sunday morning. She hadn't slept well last night. There was no Joel pressed against her. She missed the sex, but she missed the man more.

The cats followed her to the kitchen and she fed them while the coffee brewed. Then they all headed out to look over the lake. This time the duck swimming past her cottage didn't even give her a glance. No handouts here.

She opened the Sunday paper and glanced through its pages, but she couldn't concentrate. She and Joel usually yakked about the headlines with each other. She tossed it aside. She went in the house and returned with the book she was reading. She gave up on it after a half-dozen pages.

Damn. The lake usually brought her a sense of serenity, but no leg was rubbing against hers. No Joel was sitting in the Adirondack chair next to hers. She got up and stalked into the house. She opened the refrigerator and frowned. Joel fixed her eggs in the morning when she woke up hungry. She closed the door and peeked in her cupboards. No cereal. With a sigh, she slid two pieces of bread in the toaster. Back to the usual routine.

When it was time to go to her parents' house for the big Sunday meal, she didn't bother to put on makeup. What was the point? When she walked into the kitchen, her mom and sisters were laughing and talking. Good. Conversation would make the time pass.

"No Joel today?" Mom asked.

"His grand opening's tomorrow. He needed a quiet day today."

There must have been something in her tone. Her mom and sisters all zeroed in on it.

"Is everything okay between you two?" Sue-Ellen focused her full attention on her.

"Sure, we're fine."

They knew her too well. "Then what's bothering you?"

The truth spilled out. "He brought up living together, but that's a big step, so we decided to just spend our weekends together. He and Adele will be here next Sunday."

Clair frowned. "You both decided, or just you?"

"What is this, the Inquisition? I waffled, okay? Adele's a big responsibility to take on. I don't want her to think Joel and I are together when it might only be temporary."

Sue-Ellen stared at her but didn't say anything—something unheard of. Clair stared, too.

But her mom always spoke her mind. "You knew Joel and Adele were a package deal when you met him. If all you want are some romps between the sheets, you're fine, but if you want that man, you take his daughter, too. And you'd better know which you want, because Joel isn't the type who's going to be satisfied with booty calls for long. Sex is like fast food—a lot of empty calories."

Sue-Ellen put her hands on her hips. "Do you love him?"

Miriam rubbed her forehead. Maybe she should have called with a lame excuse to stay home today. "I don't know."

It was Clair's turn. "How would you feel if he decided to call the whole thing off?"

"You mean end it? No more anything?" Miriam felt coldness seep through her body. She hugged herself.

Sue-Ellen shook her head. "Yup. That hug says it all. You're nuts about the guy."

Her dad walked into the kitchen and came to her defense. "Leave her alone. How long has she known him? If Joel has any balls at all and wants her, he'll hang in there."

Did Joel want her? As a friend? A lover? What if he only wanted to live together and nothing more?

Her mother used to say *Be careful what you wish for*. That's what Miriam *thought* she wanted. But was it enough? Would it be enough for Joel? That hinted at temporary, that when the going got rough, you moved on. Could she cope with that?

Her dad wrapped an arm around her shoulders. "You're going to be fine, kid. No one said romance was easy."

No kidding. She used to laugh at the sappy romance movies that came out every year. The angst and suffering felt like soap opera antics to her. Was it really like that? Lord, save her! She might be in for a bumpy ride.

# Chapter 27

Sunday was torture for Joel. He missed Miriam. He fretted about the grand opening. He should have taken her up on her offer to go to her parents' house for their big family meal. He wouldn't be thinking the same thoughts over and over like a hamster in a wheel in his mind. Would customers come? Would they like his beer? His food? Would the bright colors, so different from everything else in Mill Pond, turn them away?

When those worries would start to subside, he'd think about Miriam. He wasn't sure how he felt about her suggestion to spend weekends together. He'd thought they were a good fit, but she'd run from the idea of living together. Maybe all she wanted him for was sex. Not that they weren't great in bed together. They were, but that wasn't what he was looking for at this stage in his life. It wasn't enough.

Adele had watched TV while he started the laundry and got a few things done around the apartment, so he said now, "Let's drive to the national park and hike a trail. It's June. It should be beautiful." He needed to get out of the apartment, to keep busy with other things besides worrying himself to death.

Hikes weren't Adele's thing, so she balked at the idea. "I'm still tired from my trip. I'd rather stay home."

He wasn't buying that, but his daughter could be stubborn when she dug in. He wasn't up to arguing with her, though, so he said, "Okay, what if we drive to Bloomington to window-shop and eat out?"

That perked her up. Her tiredness quickly fled. "Will any of the shops be open?" She loved to shop, loved knickknacks, and her allowance had gone into her account at the beginning of June, so she had money to spend.

"I can't say for sure, but let's find out. Bloomington's not that far from here, so if you see something you really want, we can always drive back to buy it."

She turned off whatever show she'd been watching and went to get ready. Joel reached for his cell phone to call Miriam to invite her to go with them, then remembered she'd be at her family get-together. The one he'd turned down. So he turned off his cell. Why had he done that? Decided to stay home? It had seemed like the responsible thing to do at the time.

Once they were ready, he helped Adele into his pickup. The first step was high and she had trouble with it, but he'd needed a pickup for the renovation work he'd used to do on the strip malls. And then they set off.

It was evening when he'd driven here with Miriam. He appreciated the rugged scenery even more in the daytime. Tyne had told him it was easy to find geodes in the rock walls and streams in the area. When he was a boy, he'd bought a geode to keep on his desk to use as a paperweight.

He drove to the center of downtown again and parked in the area that catered to college kids. It had a different energy about it than the more upscale shops near the Malibu Grill, and a few artists had set up booths on the sidewalks, peddling their wares. They walked up and down the street and stopped in a shop that sold smoothies. Adele found a picture of a guardian angel hovering over a young girl and bought it. She had a lot of angel knickknacks packed in a box to set up in her bedroom when they finally found a house.

A shopkeeper told Joel about a nearby mall. They drove there and wandered in and out of shops. Adele found a T-shirt with a line of cats across its top and bought it. Two shops later she started to limp. It happened every time she got too tired, so he said, "Let's find someplace to grab some supper. You ready?"

"Can we go back to the sandwich place in town? You get to choose your own toppings." She liked anything new. That shop had music blasting and had all kinds of mix-and-match items scribbled on the walls.

It took her a while to decide among the many choices, and when they finally sat down to eat, they couldn't hear each other speak over the music. Summer students were scattered at different tables, a few of them working on laptops while they ate their food. Adele looked around and preened, feeling part of it all. He'd have to bring her here again.

Finally, it was time to head home, and they were both ready. Halfway there, her arm started to jerk and he knew they'd overdone it a little. "Did you take your pill?" he asked. She usually watched the timing religiously, but this time she shook her head.

"I forgot."

"Better take it now, then." He always carried a bottle of water in the truck, just in case. Ten minutes later her arm relaxed.

When they got back to Mill Pond and settled in, Joel went to fold the clothes in the dryer and let her watch whatever she wanted. They'd call it an early night. They had to be up and at the brewery early tomorrow. And, thankfully, when they headed to their bedrooms, Joel was tired enough to fall to sleep instantly. Once, sometime in the night, he stretched his arm out for Miriam but then remembered she wasn't there. She wouldn't be. Only on Fridays and Saturdays and, damn it, he was going to go with that and enjoy it while it lasted.

# Chapter 28

Miriam pulled into a parking space behind the brewery on Monday morning and her pulse skipped a beat when she saw Joel's big, green pickup near the back door. She'd missed the man, damn it, couldn't wait to see him again, but there was no reason he needed to know that. She put on her kick-butt face as she walked through the door. Voices came from the kitchen, so she went there first.

Joel was working with his cook, making big pots of chili and taco meat. When he looked up and saw her, he dropped what he was doing to come straight to her and wrap her in a hug. "God, I've missed you."

Tears threatened. Her insides melted. She felt like soft cream cheese wrapped in skin. But he didn't need to know that either. She smiled and gave a small salute. "Miriam Reinhardt, reporting for duty."

He kissed the tip of her nose. "Adele's in the dining room, filling ketchup and mustard bottles. She won't last long. I'm helping to get the food ready." He motioned to the cook. "Miriam, Dave. Dave, Miriam. If you'd help Audrie with orders today, I'd appreciate it."

Miriam knew Dave. He'd almost flunked sophomore English, but he was a hard worker. He'd graduated and gone straight into working at the local plastics factory. Unfortunately, the factory had shut down two months ago. "Is Audrie here now?"

"Yup, wrapping silverware. You've probably taught her and all my counter help at one time or another. Except for Audrie, they're in high school or college and work part-time. I'm hoping Audrie might stay on if things work out well."

Joel had gotten a good worker in Audrie. Miriam had just finished teaching her youngest sister, who'd graduated in June. She'd taught all three girls in the family and liked every one of them. Audrie was twenty-three and married, with a one-year-old at home. She'd heard a lot about the new baby from Beth, her sister. He'd been a colicky little boy, fussy and demanding, but he'd been the first. The family adored him. Her mom babysat while she worked.

Miriam headed to the dining room. She passed three more girls she'd taught—Sammi, Madison, and Gia. All good girls. If Joel had hired them, he'd done a good job.

Madison, who'd just finished her second year at Bloomington, stared at her. "Are you working here, Miss Reinhardt?"

Miriam felt herself puff up with pride. "I'm helping my friend, Joel, get started. We've been seeing each other."

Madison couldn't hide her surprise. Miriam didn't blame her. No one thought Mill Pond's old-maid schoolteacher would ever hook up with a guy. "Well, it's nice seeing you."

Miriam smiled. "Nice seeing you, too." In the dining room she sidled up to Audrie—a good, solid student. Not straight As but never lower than Cs. "Joel's a friend of mine. He sent me to help you. I'm just temporary until he gets all the kinks worked out. What do you want me to do?"

Audrie nodded toward Adele. "She's a sweet girl, but she's struggling. If you can get salt and pepper shakers, sugars, and ketchup and mustard on each table, that would be great."

Miriam watched Adele and finally really understood what Joel had been trying to tell her. Even small chores were hard for the girl, but he wanted her to feel like she was part of this. Her twisted hand made it hard for her to hold the ketchup bottles while she flipped a bigger bottle over to refill them. Miriam watched for a minute, then sauntered beside her and gripped the top bottle. "Move it, lard ass. You're being a poky pants. I'll fill them if you hold them."

Adele had been looking frustrated. Now, she laughed. "We'll be a team."

It still wasn't fast, but it was better. Miriam could have done it in half the time, but by ten thirty, they had every table in the family room and bar ready to go. They'd started the coffee urns and made an urn of iced tea. Then Adele gladly scurried back to Joel's office and her beloved TV.

At eleven Joel walked to the front door and turned to look at his workers. "Are you ready?"

Everyone looked a little intimidated. A line was starting outside. They nodded, and he unlocked the brewery for business.

It was constant customers from then to the end of the night at eight. First-shift workers traded places with evening workers and the line of customers never slowed down. Friends from town came to check out the brewery, but lots and lots of tourists flocked in, too. By the end of the night everyone looked at one another and shook their heads.

Miriam worked hard as a teacher. She came home every night mentally and emotionally exhausted. But she'd never been on her feet from eight in the morning until eight at night. She thought her legs might die. She'd started out helping Audrie serve customers. They placed their orders at the front of the line, then the three girls— Sammi, Madison, and Gia—made them to order, and then the customers received them and paid for them at the end. Sounded simple, but there were so many orders, they could hardly keep up. Miriam ended up helping wherever she was needed.

Dave, the cook, grinned. "Well, I guess you don't have to worry about not having enough business, and we survived. We didn't run out of anything and everyone got good service."

Joel ran a hand through his soft, brown hair. Miriam's fingers itched. She loved the feel of his hair. He gave a soft laugh. "Everyone was curious. Maybe tomorrow won't be as rushed."

But Miriam had a feeling Joel had hit on something Mill Pond had been waiting for. And more and more tourists were finding their way here. He'd be lucky if business slowed down when the weather turned cold.

Joel gave a big smile. "We survived our grand opening. Trial by fire. Let's clean up and get out of here."

They knew what to do. Everyone cleaned their own stations, and Joel motioned to Tom, the dishwasher and custodian. "We'll stay out of your way while you sweep and mop so you can walk out with us." Tom was older, in his early forties, and had lost his job when the plastics factory closed. While everyone else scrubbed and sterilized, Joel wrapped up the paperwork for the night, and Miriam went to check on Adele. In an hour everyone was ready to leave.

When they finally walked out the door and locked up for the night, she leaned against Joel as he walked her to her car. "I've had it. I'm pooped. I need to go home to my cats, but I'll be back tomorrow morning."

He pulled her in for a kiss before he opened her car door for her.

"Thanks for all the help. You made things go a lot smoother. I appreciate it."

She pursed her lips. "You've done a good thing here. You've provided some good people with good jobs. They needed them. And you'll bring even more tourists into Mill Pond."

He looked uncomfortable. "I feel sort of guilty hiring such solid people because they lost their jobs at the factory, but my pay isn't much off what the factory paid them. It isn't a high-wage place to work."

He was such a nice person! Miriam reached out and hugged him. "They're just glad they aren't going to lose their houses and have to move somewhere else to find work."

He pressed his lips together and nodded. "Did you know Maya's going to work here two nights a week?"

"My Maya?"

"Is there any other?" Joel laughed at her and she blushed.

"After all Hazel's done for her, is she leaving her on her own at the day care center to work here?"

"Nope. There weren't any kids in the evenings, and Hazel liked that. She can manage the rest during the days and have her evenings to herself."

Miriam's thoughts returned to Maya and Joel shook his head.

"What now? She's starting college this fall, but your wheels are still turning; I can tell."

He always caught her out. He was too damned intuitive. "I still think that girl would like accounting more than teaching."

"Then I'm sure you'll mention it." Joel ran a finger over her cheek and a thrill shot through her. "You're pretty damned special. Now go home and get some sleep. I'll see you tomorrow."

She was so tired, she could hardly move. She'd fall asleep the minute her head hit the pillow. But she still wanted him in bed next to her. That would have to wait, though. Her own fault. But this had better be temporary. If she had to throw herself on her knees and beg him to move in with her, she just might.

# Chapter 29

For the next few days Joel tweaked things at the work stations. Business never slowed down, so he hired two more part-time people—one to work with Audrie during the day and another to work with Faith when she took Audrie's place in the evenings. The two guys he'd hired to work in the brewery started out smooth and just kept getting better. He was selling so much beer, he considered setting up two more tanks.

His beer guys had ideas about that, too.

"I think we should do a citrusy beer," Collin urged. He'd dropped out of college in his second year—hated number crunching—and had worked his way up to being a bartender in Bloomington since then, but he really wanted to move home. The job pickings were slim, though, so when his mom had read the ads for the brewery, she'd called him and he'd come for an interview. Joel considered himself lucky to get him.

"The light beers went over with girls in college." Collin said. "When girls frequent a place, guys come. They won't hang out in the family room, but you have a neat bar. They'd come here." He grinned.

Casey, his best friend at Mill Pond High, who'd worked lots of odd jobs before applying here, nodded. "I'd like us to make a beer with a lot of foam, a good head. Some people look for that."

They discussed ingredients and decided to make a few buckets of home brew in the back room where they bottled the beer. The guys impressed Joel with their enthusiasm and knowledge, so he crossed off the brewery as something to worry about.

The only disappointment he'd had so far was Ross, the guy he'd hired to be his right-hand man. He came to work when he felt like it. He hadn't been on time once since the brewery opened. He always had an excuse. He was having car trouble. His girlfriend broke her toe and he had to drive her to emergency care. His alarm clock didn't go off. Finally, Joel called him into his office and sent Adele to help Miriam for a while.

He spread his hands. "Do you want this job or not? I need someone who can take my place when I want a day off, someone I can count on. So far, Miriam's been my troubleshooter. She fills in wherever someone needs her, but she's doing me a favor. She won't be here next week. You have to kick in. When the tour bus pulled in and we looked for you, you were on break."

Ross looked down and shook his head. "It's been a rough start, man. I didn't mean to let you down. I'd really like to make as much money as I can before I start school again in the fall."

"That's what you told me, that you're a business major and you'd like some experience. You can get it here, but you have to commit. If you're late one more time, I have to let you go."

But later that day, when there was a lull in business and Joel went to get Adele and Miriam to hide at a private picnic table behind the building to eat together, he had to search for Ross to cover for him. He found him, standing by a friend's car in the parking lot, visiting with his buddies.

Ross hurried to meet him and asked, "What's up?"

Joel shook his head. "I'm taking an hour break. I need you inside."

"I'm on it." And Ross disappeared into the building.

Once he and Miriam arranged their food on the picnic table and got Adele settled, Miriam looked at him. "I hope you have a backup person in mind to take Ross's place. The kid's smart enough. As came easy for him, but he has no motivation. His dad runs an insurance company in town and Ross will work with him when he graduates from college. I was surprised to see him here, but then Leona . . ."

"The hairdresser married to Garth?" Joel asked.

She nodded. "When I got my hair cut, she told me that Ross's dad told him no more free ride at college. He's blowing through too much money, so no extras for partying until he got a job."

Joel tilted his head to the side and studied her. "Is that why your hair looks curlier?"

She blinked. "My hair has nothing to do with Ross."

"You got it cut. I like how bouncy it is now."

She rolled her eyes. "I get it cut every five weeks. I've had the same hairstyle since I started teaching. Now, get back on topic. We were talking about Ross."

Joel sighed. "I get it. He's just working to please Daddy. Everything comes too easy for him." He'd gotten that impression when he'd interviewed him. "The thing is, no one else applied for that position. Collin would be a great manager, but he loves working in the brewery."

Miriam finished her Coney dog and fries, then turned to smile at Adele. "This might not be the best time to tell you, but Adele and I have decided we want to have a sleepover—a girls' night out—at my place tonight. We'd like to leave here early and buy a pizza and watch *Beauty and the Beast* while we paint our finger- and toenails."

"Bless you."

Miriam blinked, not expecting that response. Joel walked to where she sat and hugged her. He'd hired an extra server for the evening shift, when things always got busier, and things were running smoothly. "I've spent as much time as I can with Adele, but I know she's been stuck in my office too long. And you've worked too many hours here. You're a saint."

She laughed. "No one's ever accused me of that before and I don't intend to live up to it, but we need out of this place and we're sick of hot dogs."

Joel grinned. "Tell you what. Why don't you two sleep in tomorrow and I'll have Ross prep the tables? You don't need to show up until we're ready to open the doors."

"Sounds good to me. I'm taking her to my parents' get-together on Sunday, too. I know you're swamped right now, but you're invited to hang out with us on Friday and Saturday nights if you want to."

"If I want to?" He clutched her hand. "You have no idea how much I've missed you. I mean, I know you're here, but . . ."

She waved away his explanation. "I get it. I know. Me too."

That was what he liked about her. He'd spent half his married life coddling April, lifting her up. Miriam didn't need to be coddled. Hell, she was doing her best to lift *him* up. "Lord, I love you."

The words had slipped out and he immediately wished he could take them back. He'd meant to say *I love everything about you*, but there, he'd blurted out his true feelings, right after she'd let him know she wanted to take it slow. She'd probably run for the hills now.

Instead, she locked gazes with him and said, "I love you, too, idiot. I just don't want to rush things. I've been alone a long time."

It was a bone and he'd take it. She liked being around him, liked *him*, and he wouldn't push her. Warmth spread inside him. She loved him. She'd said it. They were going to be all right.

Adele stared at them. "You two are in love?" The girl spent half her life watching romances on the Hallmark Channel. The sappier the story, the more she liked it. They must not fit her idea of romance.

Miriam arched an eyebrow at her. "We sure are, but love's different at our age. We're smarter about it."

Adele frowned. She wasn't quite sure how to interpret that. Hell, she was just a kid. Joel wasn't quite sure about it himself. He just knew it felt wonderful. He reached over to tousle her blond hair. "You can't always predict how things will play out, kid, but one thing I do know. A business won't run itself, so we have to get back to work."

She wrinkled her nose at him. "Do we have to?"

"Sure do. Work first . . ."

". . . play later." She'd heard it before, over and over again.

When they walked back into the building, it was business as usual, but after the evening supper shift, Miriam and Adele waved early good-byes and took off. Joel watched them pull away, grateful and worried at the same time. He hoped they'd bond, that they'd really enjoy each other. He didn't expect anyone to love Adele the way he did, but if Miriam could just care about her as much as she did Maya, he'd be happy. For tonight, though, his daughter needed attention, and Miriam had stepped up to the plate again.

The rest of the night flew by. Ian and Tessa came with their little boy, Drew, and Joel took a few minutes to sit at their table.

There was no missing them in the family room, even with all the tourists. Ian was tall, dark, and handsome. Tessa's mass of long, copper curls made her stand out anywhere. Ian gestured at the bright colored walls and metal beams. "What a fun place. It's perfect for Mill Pond. We don't have anything else like it."

Tessa gestured at Drew in his high chair, happily grabbing French fries and pieces of a hot dog she'd cut up for him. "It's a great place to bring kids. So much is going on, he doesn't know whether to eat or watch the people around him."

Ian held up the glass of lager he'd ordered. "I'll be coming back for more of this. Damn, it's good."

Joel had to leave after a few minutes to help bus tables in the brewery. Jordan could keep up at the dishwasher as long as someone got the dishes *to* him, but things were so busy, no one could get to it. As Joel hustled dirty glasses to the kitchen, he felt good that Ian and Tessa had liked his place. Harley and Kathy had come for supper on Tuesday night and liked it, too.

By closing time he was ahead of schedule. He'd already grabbed the days' receipts from each cash register and locked the money in the safe. He even had each cash register filled with money to start the next day. He hadn't realized how much not having Adele here would free him up. He didn't have to run to check on her every chance he got. He could concentrate his full attention on the business at hand. And when he locked up to leave, for the first time in a long time, he'd be going home alone. He stopped at Art's and bought a steak and a bag of salad. He felt guilty, making it for himself when Miriam and Adele were eating pizza, but God, it tasted good. He thought he'd hate watching TV by himself, but he was so tired, he found it was a relief. No old movie or Disney special. He sank onto his couch and turned on the Discovery Channel. He couldn't remember the last time he'd watched something *he* picked. He fell asleep before the show ended. He woke on the couch when his phone alarm went off.

Had he really slept a full eight hours? He felt wonderful, rejuvenated. And it was all thanks to Miriam.

# Chapter 30

On Friday Joel was working with Dave in the kitchen when someone knocked on the back door and stepped inside. The buzzer went off and Joel glanced at the security screen to see who'd arrived early for work. Not an employee: Miles. Footsteps sounded in the hallway and Joel froze for a second. He was already pushed for time. He'd told Miriam and Adele to sleep in, that he'd have Ross do setup this morning, but Ross had yet to show up. Joel suspected he didn't intend to . . . ever again.

Miles glanced in the kitchen and stopped when he saw Joel. He looked down at his feet, wouldn't meet Joel's eyes. "Can we talk?"

Joel put on a smile. "Sure; let's go in my office." He glanced at Dave. Dave had to see the similarities between them—the same coloring and build, except for Joel's potbelly—but he didn't ask questions, just gave Joel a thumbs-up.

"I'm in good shape. No worries."

Joel led Miles down the hallway and held his office door for him, shutting it behind them once they were inside. He turned to his brother with a frown. "You lost your job?"

"It's not what you think. I stayed sober until they let the whole custodial staff go. They decided to go with an outside crew that was cheaper. They won't have to pay benefits that way either." Miles grimaced. "They'll get what they deserve. No more quality work, just the basics."

Joel's anger left as quickly as it had come. "I'm sorry. You liked that job."

"Employers don't give a shit about workers anymore. I lost it for a minute, bought a bottle to make me feel better, but I didn't want to move back in with Mom and Dad. When they told me about your new place, I thought I'd come here to look for a job."

Joel studied him. "Are you sober now?"

"Yup. Have been since Monday. I don't want to go that route again."

Miles's voice had an edge to it that Joel hadn't heard for a long time. He nodded. "My assistant manager didn't show today. I could use someone to bounce around wherever he's needed. Have you ever managed before?"

"I was over the entire crew at the factory."

Joel blinked. He hadn't known that. "Perfect; then you should be fine. Let's see what you've got." He hesitated. "I bought a trailer and put it across the parking lot, near the trees, in case you needed a place to stay."

Miles stared at him. "For me?"

"But you can only work in the brewery as long as you have your shit together. Is this the right place for you? Will the beer tempt you too much?"

Miles pulled a face. "I hate beer, only drink the hard stuff. But I'm done with that, too. I hope."

He was being honest. That made Joel feel better. No false confidence. His brother knew he'd have to work to stay clean, probably for the rest of his life.

"I joined AA when I got the job at the factory, didn't want to drink it away. I've learned I can't beat my demons myself. I need help."

"If you can hold it together, you and I could manage this place together as a team. Nothing would make me happier." Being with Miriam would make him *as* happy, though. That was for sure. "Come on. I'll show you the trailer. You can move in after we close up tonight." He opened his desk drawer and pressed a key into Miles's hand.

They crossed the parking lot and long yard to the double-wide. Miles opened the door and shook his head. He closed his eyes for a second and took a deep breath. "You even furnished it. You bought a big-screen TV."

"Welcome home, Bro." Miles looked like he might break down, so Joel said, "You'll have to enjoy all this later. Right now, I plan to work you to death. You need to learn the ropes."

Miles squared his shoulders. "I'm ready to dig in."

Joel introduced him to everyone and explained that Ross was a no-show and his brother had come to help out.

"Where should I start?" Miles asked.

"With setup. Ask Audrie. She'll put you to work." He led him to the food counter and handed him over to her, then left them to it. It had been hard for Miles to make himself come here, he knew. He'd give him some time to adjust.

When Miriam and Adele walked through the doors before he opened for business, Miriam stared at the tables and smiled. "Thanks for asking Ross to fill in for us. We've had a great time."

They stood side by side, bumping shoulders. They looked happy with each other. Relief swam through his veins. They must have had a good night.

Joel wrapped an arm around her. The world should know how he felt about her. "Ross never showed. My brother did. He's fast and efficient." He motioned to Miles, wrapping silverware at the counter. Adele laughed when she saw him and opened her arms for a hug. Miles went to her and wrapped her in a close embrace. "Hello, Sunshine!"

He'd always called her that because of her bright blond hair. Then he turned to Miriam. "We were never formally introduced. I'm Miles."

"And I'm Miriam." She'd been watching him closely. "I'm glad you're here."

"About my parents' house . . ."

"You didn't expect to see us. You were a little under the weather, but you look better now."

He smiled. "I *am* better now. Thank you."

Joel looked at Miriam, amazed by her as usual. "That was nice."

She shrugged. "He wants this to work. So do you. We'll all do what we can to help it along."

Joel looked at the clock, then, and walked to the doors to open them. There was a line, as usual. More and more tourists were stopping there before they went from shop to shop in town. Joel had worried he was taking away business from Ralph's Diner, but Tyne told him Ralph's was full, too.

"Everybody's busy," Miriam told him. "Chase had to hire Louise's daughter to help with the outside tables. He and Harley trade off using the college kids to work their bars so they can get a couple nights off a week. Ian's resort is full, every room taken for the rest of the season. A few people in town are talking about converting their big, old houses into bed-and-breakfasts."

Miles looked surprised. "Sounds like they'd be hitting at the right time."

People crowded the counters, so there was no more time to talk. They hurried to wait on the customers. Joel was happy to see Miles had a natural, easy style to keeping things flowing. He was ten times better than Ross, without training, on his first day. When there was a short lull at three thirty, Joel invited him to join him, Adele, and Miriam for a quick lunch on the back patio.

"I love your Reuben dog," Miles said, biting into his second one. "I noticed every choice seemed to sell well."

Joel couldn't keep the pride from his voice. "I'm pretty happy about that. Tyne helped me, though. He's one of the chefs at the Lakeview Stables Resort."

"You have enough variety to keep customers coming back for more." Miles looked at Miriam. "Are you going to work here all summer?"

She shook her head. "Nah. I was just backup in case there were start-up problems. That, and I wanted to keep an eye on Joel to make sure no pretty young things were hitting on my man."

Adele's jaw dropped. "Would you be jealous? Of Dad?" She couldn't seem to wrap her mind around the idea.

Miriam finished her beer and chuckled. "Hell yes. That's part of being in love."

Miles stared. "When did you guys get serious?"

Miriam didn't wait for Joel to answer. "While Adele was on the trip with her grandma and grandpa."

"And you're in love?" Miles sounded as surprised as Adele had been. No one had expected Joel to find someone else, including him.

Miriam's blue eyes sparkled. "It's too soon to be sure, but we sure like each other a lot."

Miles finished his root beer and gave his brother a small punch on the arm. "Good for you! It's Friday, man. Why don't you let me finish up here after supper so you can leave early? Go have some fun."

"Not tonight." It was too soon. "But I might take you up on that tomorrow night, once I walk you through closing and locking up. Eventually, I'd like to take a day or two off. That's why I hired an assistant manager. And then I can cover so you can take time off, too. Mill Pond is a great place for a fresh start. You'll see."

Miles ran a hand over his forehead, looking bemused.

Joel knew how he felt. He sort of felt that way, too. Nothing in life ever came this easy. "Things are falling into place," he said. "We'll get there. Between the two of us, this place will run like clockwork." That's what he hoped for, what he wanted.

Miles nodded. "I think so, too, but who'd have thought?"

*Exactly.*

Adele looked worried. "You're still going to spend the night with Miriam and me, aren't you, Dad?"

"Are you kidding? I can't wait. I'll just get to her house a little later than you do."

Satisfied with his answer, Adele looked at Miles. "Can I spend the night at your trailer sometime?"

"Would you like that?" He sounded hopeful.

"Will you watch *Grease* with me?" She knew better than to ask him to watch a Disney movie.

He laughed. "I could force myself to watch Olivia Newton-John in skintight black pants."

Miriam rolled her eyes. "Men!"

They were still laughing when they walked back into the brewery and got to work. Miriam and Adele stayed until after the supper rush and then headed to Miriam's cottage. Joel led Miles to his office and showed him where the safe was and how he kept his books.

"If you just throw the receipts for the day in the safe with the money, I can do the rest in the morning."

"You didn't show this to the young kid who just quit, did you?"

Joel gave him a look. "Hell no."

"But you showed it to me? On the first day on the job. Aren't you worried at all? What if I backslide and need money for booze?"

Joel caught and held his gaze. "Have you ever stolen before in your life?"

"No."

"Then why would you steal from me? Give yourself some credit, Miles. You've made some mistakes, just like I did. Let's move past them."

"Maybe it scares me when things feel too good."

"You think you're the only one? I can hardly believe Miriam

wants anything to do with me. I can hardly believe I opened the doors of this place for business and customers showed up. I'm still pinching myself."

Miles stared at him. "I thought it was just me."

"Get over yourself. Start thinking that life can get better. It just might."

They went back on the floor to help finish for the night. Business didn't slow down until closing at eight. Maybe a good thing. They didn't have a chance to worry. A lot of customers stayed right up until last call. Then they left to go to Chase's bar or Harley's winery.

"If you wanted to, you could stay busy lots later on the brewery side," Miles said.

Joel glanced at Collin and Casey. "They work long-enough hours. I'd rather start slow and add more employees a little at a time."

Miles nodded. "Ease into things. That's what I'm going to do."

When the last person walked out of the building, Joel showed his brother his routine for closing and locking up. He introduced him to how to set the security system, too. Then he said, "I have a spare key for your trailer if you lose yours. If you look in the cupboards and freezer when you get home, I stocked up a few things for you. There are some frozen TV dinners and breakfast burritos, and there's toilet paper, soap, and toothpaste in the bathroom."

"Home." Miles shook his head. "Thanks for everything, Joel. I never expected . . ." He looked away and started toward his truck. He stopped and looked back at his brother. "You won't regret this."

"I'm not worried about that. It's going to be nice being in business together."

Miles opened his truck door and ran a hand over his face, visibly fighting for composure. "It's going to be great."

Joel gave a wave and drove away. Miriam and Adele would be waiting for him.

# Chapter 31

When Miriam settled Adele in her old Mercedes and started to her cottage, she paused at the edge of the brewery's parking lot. "We get to go home and relax, but your dad always stays and works till the very end. I'd like to make him something fun to eat when he gets home tonight. He has to be as tired of hot dogs as we are."

Adele's forehead crinkled in thought. "We don't know how to cook."

"Well, that's a problem, but groceries have frozen food sections, don't they? And stuff that's convenient and easy."

"A cake?" Adele always went for dessert.

"No, something that will stick to his ribs, the kind of food his mom makes, but it has to be simple."

"Grandma can make anything," Adele said.

"Yeah, that's why we have to cheat." Miriam stopped at Art's Grocery and told him her predicament. "I don't cook. It has to be something I can't mess up." She'd thought about calling Tyne, but as a chef, he never made anything that didn't take a cupboard full of ingredients. "Do you have anything I can make?" she asked Art.

He grinned. "I have you covered. For a while I advertised a recipe a week, featuring ingredients I put on special with a sale price. I wanted it to be just a few easy steps. Customers loved it, but my Mary got sick of trying to think of ideas for it, so it fizzled. She still makes the chicken and dumpling recipe she came up with, though, and it's delicious."

"How many steps?" Miriam asked.

"She simplified the recipe from one of her favorite cookbooks— *In the Kitchen with David* by David Venable—until even a monkey could make it." He grinned. "Not that I'm comparing you to one."

She shrugged. "Wouldn't bother me. A monkey might be better in the kitchen. I need a dump-and-stir recipe."

"Then this one's for you."

He grabbed a brown grocery sack and a marker, then began to write down the recipe. "First, oil the bottom of a Dutch oven."

She stopped him. "A what?"

"A big pan with tall sides you use to make soups and stews."

"I've got one of those."

"Good. Heat the oil, then add a bag of frozen mirepoix." He saw her look and said, "A bag of frozen diced onions, carrots, and celery."

"In your freezer section?"

"With the vegetables. Sauté those until they're tender, then add a bag of frozen, diced, cooked chicken breasts. I stock those close to the frozen chicken nuggets. Add some salt and pepper and let them cook until they start to brown. Now, add a sprinkle of dried parsley, a sprinkle of dried thyme, and two bay leaves."

She frowned.

"They're in the spice section, above the kosher salt. After you stir those in, pour in a thirty-two-ounce box of chicken broth."

"That's by the soups?"

He nodded. "When everything gets hot, pop open a tube of flaky biscuits, flatten each one on a floured board, cut them into bite-sized pieces, and drop them in the soup. Mary didn't use the whole tube, just added as many as she wanted. Turn the heat down and let the dumplings cook through. They're going to puff up a lot. Then take out the bay leaves and you're ready to go."

She glanced at Adele. "We can do that, right?"

Adele nodded, but then, Adele was always optimistic. She thought the adults she loved could do anything.

Art pointed to the dairy case. "The biscuits are there." He handed Miriam the grocery bag with the recipe written on it. "Good luck."

Miriam was optimistic until the drive home. Then she wondered what the hell she'd been thinking. But Art was right; she'd never find an easier recipe than this. It truly was a dump-and-stir. And if worse came to worse, she'd bought a chocolate cake.

Tommy and Tuppence were excited when she and Adele carried the plastic grocery bags into the kitchen. They sulked when no cans of cat food came out of them, but they purred when Miriam opened the bag of frozen, diced chicken and dumped it in the pan. Once the pieces cooked through, she scooped out a few of them for each cat. Maybe a mistake. They wove themselves around her ankles, begging for more.

Adele was the designated stir person.

"Be careful when I pour in the broth. Don't splash yourself," Miriam warned.

When Miriam popped the biscuit tube, Adele had fun pressing each biscuit in flour on both sides while Miriam cut them. By the time they'd finished, the broth was hot, and they started to drop the small squares of dough into the mix.

"Look!" Miriam watched as the dough puffed up and soaked up some of the liquid. "They're getting big."

They'd barely finished before Joel walked into the cottage. They glanced at each other, proud of themselves. He sniffed and raised his eyebrows. "What's up? Something smells wonderful in here."

Miriam lifted the lid and pointed. "Adele and I made chicken and dumplings for you."

He backed away, nervous.

"I tried them, Dad. They're good," Adele said. "We've been waiting to eat with you."

"You waited? That was nice of you. Let's dig in." He went into the kitchen to sit at the small table for four. Miriam plopped the Dutch oven on a trivet in the center and handed each of them a bowl. "Bon appétit!"

Joel eyed it warily and dished up. She watched him screw up his courage. He took a bite and blinked.

"Is it good?" She waited for him to swallow.

"It's better than good. I love it." He dipped in for more.

She was encouraged enough to try some, too. She'd never once liked anything she'd made so hadn't been brave enough, but bless Art's Grocery. This was a winner. She felt herself swell with pride. Finally, she'd made something edible. Maybe grilling hot dogs at the brewery was expanding her horizons. She'd have to go back to Art's and beg for all the recipes his Mary had come up with for the sale specials.

They all had seconds before they started cleanup. The meal was a little heavy for this late at night, but they'd been so hungry for real food, they didn't care. They settled in the living room to watch TV and relax.

"Guess what, Dad?" Adele could hardly contain herself. "Miriam bought a big-screen TV and mounted it on the wall in my bedroom."

Joel shook his head. He turned to Miriam. "That's too expensive. Let me pay you back for that."

"Not gonna happen." She reached for Adele's hand. "That was my house-welcoming present for her."

Joel looked at their clasped hands and got an odd expression on his face. "Are you two ganging up against me?"

Adele leaned forward and kissed his cheek. "It's all about girl power, Dad."

Instead of laughing, he looked so emotional, it surprised Miriam. "Are you all right?"

He gave a quick nod. His voice sounded hoarse. "It's just nice that you two get along so well."

Then she understood. He'd been worried that she'd only tolerate Adele, never feel close to her. "You've had too many worries in your life," she told him, "but Adele and I get along fine."

Adele yawned and stood. "I'm tired. I'm going to watch my new TV and go to sleep." She wasn't fooling anyone. She was so excited about having her own TV in her room, she couldn't wait to try it out.

When she left them and closed her bedroom door, Miriam turned to Joel. "You must be tired, too. Ready for bed?"

He clicked off the TV in the living room and grinned. "I've had a big day. I need to relax before I can sleep. Got anything in mind?"

*Relax. Hallelujah!* She'd been dying to jump his bones, but the man looked exhausted. "Are you sure? I don't want to be too needy."

"Woman, that's one of the reasons I love you. April never wanted to have sex. If you kill me with abundance, I'll die happy."

She tugged him to his feet. "Then let's find out how healthy your heart really is." And to her amazement, it was stronger than she'd ever expected. When he finally rolled over, she spooned herself against him. She pressed her nose against the back of his neck and whispered, "I want this every night. I've missed you."

He pushed up on to an elbow and turned to look at her. "Are you asking me to move in with you?"

"Yes."

He bent his head to kiss her. "I love you, Miriam."

She gave him a lazy grin. "I love you, too. Now roll over and go to sleep. You work tomorrow and I don't want you to be too tired when you come home."

He chuckled. "I'd argue, but I've already given you about all I can tonight." He sank back onto the mattress and she snuggled close again.

Before drifting to sleep, she smiled. No more empty bed. She could reach for Joel seven nights a week now. And that felt good.

# Chapter 32

Miles was already in the dining room when Joel walked into the brewery. He looked at the tables, ready to go.

"Damn. When did you get here? Every ketchup bottle and shaker is already filled."

Miles shrugged. "I woke up early, ate one of your breakfast burritos, and decided I might as well get started for the day."

"This is great, but it means you need more in your life than working at the brewery. I need to get you out and introduce you to some people."

"That'll come. One step at a time. Don't rush me."

Dave walked in then and looked around. "You both beat me here. I must be getting slow."

Joel shook his head. "No, my brother thinks he's turning into roboboy, that he can work all hours. Eventually, he'll settle down."

"Might take some time. I lost myself in work for a period in my life. It made me happy. Whatever does the trick."

Miles studied Dave. The man was tall and gaunt, with streaks of gray at his temples. "Where did you cook before you came here?"

"I was the line cook for breakfast and lunch at the plastics factory that folded, but I've moved around a lot, going from place to place."

"Do you like Mill Pond?"

"Yup. I'm older now, thinking of settling down, and Mill Pond's a good place to be."

Joel listened with interest. Dave was still a mystery to him. When his name came up, everyone said they liked him, but no one really knew much about him, and he'd lived here for two years. By then, Mill Pond had usually absorbed you by osmosis, turned you into a friend, but Dave seemed to be a bit of a loner.

"Have you always cooked?" Miles asked.

Dave nodded. "Started out as a chef in a big restaurant in Miami, but I burned out. Now, I don't want that kind of pressure." He glanced at the clock. "It's time I get cooking. Customers don't like to wait for their food."

Joel glanced at Miles as Dave left and shrugged. "That's more than he's ever told me before, but he's a good worker. I hope he stays a long time."

"Would you mind if I went back to work with him in the kitchen before we open? I'd like to learn a little about how to cook. I've got no skills."

Joel waved him after Dave. "Go for it. I have a few things I can get done in my office."

Miriam and Adele arrived at ten thirty, and once Joel got Adele settled, he went to open the brewery's doors. Miles came, too, to pitch in wherever he was needed.

Joel and Miles worked well together. Growing up, they'd always been a great team. Then Joel married April, and two years later Miles had joined the military. When he came home from overseas, he was a different person. Joel didn't know what had happened to him, but he knew it wasn't good. He never asked about it and Miles never brought it up, but he drank heavily. And just kept drinking more.

Saturday started busy and stayed that way. Lots of tourists dragged kids into the family room or sat at the outside patio. No one got a break, and Joel thanked Miriam over and over again for coming. He'd definitely underestimated how many employees he needed for the weekends. He'd have to hire a couple more people.

They didn't catch their breaths until after supper, and then the families slowed down and more people crowded into the bar.

Joel went to find Miriam. "If you want to duck out of here now with Adele, go for it. Miles and I can cover the traffic, but I might get home later than usual."

She turned and grinned at him. "Home?"

That flustered him. What had he been thinking? "Sorry, I meant your place."

She put both hands over her heart. The woman had a flair for the dramatic. He got a kick out of that. "I love it that you think of it as home."

Before he could stop himself, the words popped out. "It's where you are." It was that simple for him.

Her curls askew from the busy day, she blew him a kiss. "See you at home." Then she hurried to his office to grab Adele and take off.

Miles and Joel went to help in the bar. Casey and Collin sighed with relief when they saw them. Joel started helping with drink orders and Miles assisted Gia at the food counter. He'd just rung up nachos for an entire table when he looked up and saw a soldier with an artificial leg limp in with a few friends.

Miles froze, locked in place, staring at the man in uniform with the missing leg. All the color drained from his face. Joel rushed to him and laid his hand on his arm. "You okay?"

Miles shook his head, as if coming out of a daze. He blinked. "Sorry; got lost for a minute in my own thoughts."

It was more than that. "Do you need a break?"

Miles turned his head away from the group. "No, I'm okay, but I need to zip into the kitchen for more chili. Our station's almost out. Will you cover for me for a second?"

"Will do."

One of the guys at the soldier's table came to give Joel their order. Another one of his friends went to get beer for the group. Miles didn't return until the table was served. No one but Dave noticed how much the soldier had shaken him. He was still pale but back on track.

When Joel ran to the kitchen for oranges for the bar, Dave asked, "Has your brother had anything to eat?"

Miles heard him and called, "We're close to quitting time. I'll be fine."

Dave handed a plate of cheese and crackers to Joel. "Make your brother eat a few of these."

Joel plopped them near Miles. "You heard the man. Eat."

Miles looked like he was going to argue, then glanced at Dave and changed his mind.

The bar didn't empty until a little after nine. People who'd ordered at eight thirty stayed to finish their food. The soldier and his friends left while Miles was in the kitchen, and Joel was grateful Miles didn't have to see him again.

It took another hour to get everything cleaned up and the receipts and cash stashed and recorded. When the last employee left the building, Joel and Miles stepped out after them, and Miles locked up. Joel asked, "Want to talk about it?"

Miles shuffled his feet. "Not much to say. My friends and I were walking down a road in Afghanistan and a stray dog ran up to us, so thin you could count its ribs. I stopped to pet it and my friends walked on. Juan stepped on a mine and they all died but Wade. He lost his leg. That dog saved my life. I adopted it, and when I left, a new guy was happy to get him."

Joel stared, at a loss for words. Finally, he asked, "Have you told anyone else about this?"

"Didn't want to. I've never understood why I didn't die. I mean, why spare me? Juan had a wife and a five-month-old son at home. He should have been the one who lived, not me."

Joel crossed his arms and looked across the empty parking lot. "I quit asking myself *why* a long time ago. I never found any answers. Now, I just try to be the best I can be and to make the most of what I have."

"But why me?" Miles asked. "I feel like I should do something with my life, but I have no idea what."

"Maybe you were supposed to bail me out when I opened a brewery and needed someone to cover my back."

Miles blinked at him. "Maybe. Maybe we were supposed to get together and mend."

"That works for me." Joel gave him a half hug. "It's not your fault your friends died. You didn't plant that mine. You survived, so say *thank you* and move on."

Miles looked grim. "Easier said than done."

Joel barked a laugh. "Who said life would be easy?" He climbed in his pickup and gave Miles a quick wave. On the drive to Miriam's, he pushed thoughts of his past out of his mind. It didn't pay to dwell on them. Miles needed to move on, too, but that would take some time.

When he pulled into Miriam's drive, looked through the window, and saw her stand and walk to the door to greet him, his dark mood lifted. He'd share this with Miriam and it would lighten the burden. With her by his side, he could do anything. He hoped Mill Pond would offer Miles the fresh start it had offered him. His brother needed it.

# Chapter 33

When Miriam drove Adele to the brewery on Saturday, she realized that, in theory, this was her last day of work. She'd volunteered to help Joel for his opening week and she had. He didn't expect her on Sunday. He didn't open the doors for business until noon then, and he knew she went to her parents' every week for the family get-together. She'd take Adele with her and, eventually, Joel meant to take Sundays off, too. Miles was eager to manage a day by himself. Miriam liked popping into Joel's world and pitching in, she just didn't want to do it every day.

She told Joel that when he came to greet her and Adele, who, as usual, went straight to her comfy chair in the office and switched on the TV. Miriam had kept her busy all morning. She'd dragged her on a short walk, then they'd tidied up the cottage.

"That girl needs to move more," Miriam told Joel.

"I know. I feel bad about that. It's just hard for me when I work."

"Well, she's got me now." She frowned. "When school starts, though, that will end. I'll be busy every day, too."

"I'll start bringing her to work with me again," Joel said.

"She just hides in your office and watches TV." She shook her head. "We'll make the best of it somehow. We'll think of something." And that's when she realized she was starting to think of them together long term. But there it was. She couldn't picture a future without Joel.

He looked all mushy and Miriam shook her head. "Concentrate. I like coming here, being a part of this, but only a few times a week. I still like to garden and read, and when school starts, I'm done."

"Simple," he said. "Chase told me Mondays are always slow at the bar, so stay home. Chase only offers lunches on Wednesdays—

his famous barbecue—and people flood the bar, so take Wednesdays off, too. Fridays and Saturdays, it would be great having you here."

She grinned. "So what if I work Tuesdays, Fridays, and Saturdays for a while?"

"Perfect; with you, the food side should be okay. And when the weather turns bad, things will slow down. Not as many tourists."

She nodded and started to the dining room. Audrie would put her to work. She called back, "You're expecting to be slammed today, right?"

"It's a beautiful Saturday, perfect weather. This will be a trial by fire."

Three hours later she had to admit he'd been right. The doors opened and people swarmed inside like locusts. For half an hour they were overwhelmed. There were a few glitches here and there, but they never totally floundered. In theory, with people lining up at the counter to give their orders and moving down the line to receive them and pay, Joel's system seemed pretty foolproof, but the line never stopped. Still, they survived.

Joel came to check on them at two. "You okay?"

Audrie grinned. "With Miriam, Sammi, and Madison? A piece of cake."

"Yeah right. The bar side barely kept its head above water. People were doing tastings, and ordering beer and food. It was organized chaos. Miles meant to float from place to place, but Gia couldn't have handled everything on her own."

Customers were still drifting in. Three-fourths of the tables were taken. Audrie took a deep breath. "It's going to be even worse to-night."

"Maybe not." Miriam looked out the side window and waved at Hank and Sadie, who sat at a table on the patio with his Chihuahua, Chester. Joel bought all his buns from Hank's bread shop. No one else's could compare to his baked goods. He special-made poppy seed and pretzel hot dog buns for the brewery. "Harley's doing a wine party tonight, with music and hors d'oeuvres. A lot of people will be going to that. Steph and Hank are catering the food and it should be fun."

"Maybe that will save us." Joel looked relieved. "We'll have more help next weekend. We've lived and learned."

Audrie gave him a sideways glance. "My middle sister's twenty-one and after hearing how much I like it here, she'd like to work here, too, in the bar."

"In the bar?"

"Someday she'd like to be a bartender."

"Will you vouch for her? Is she a good worker?"

"Our whole family works hard. She has a part-time job in the next town and they keep promising her more hours but never give them to her. Then they don't have to give her any benefits. She's looking for something else."

"She's hired. I need someone who's twenty-one. Most of the girls who apply are in high school and college, not old enough to serve drinks."

Audrie beamed. "When can she start?"

"The sooner the better."

Audrie chuckled. "Kelly might be here on Tuesday, then. She told me when she found something better, she'd go in and tell her boss it's her last day. He hasn't played fair with her, so she doesn't owe him anything."

Miriam glanced out the window. Hank was waiting to pay for his and Sadie's food at the counter. "Things have slowed down enough; I'm going to go out to say hi to Hank and Sadie."

Joel nodded. "Grab something and take your lunch break, if you want to."

She carried two Coney dogs out to join Hank as he returned to Sadie with their order. "Hey, I haven't seen you two for a while." She looked at Sadie. "Who's covering for you at your frozen custard shop?"

"Steph. She and Hank worked right through lunch to get the hors d'oeuvres done. I babysat Chester so they wouldn't have to worry about him, so she's dishing up cones so we can grab some food." It had been Steph's idea to team up with Hank to cater parties.

"Sounds fair." Hank and Sadie were both eccentric, but Miriam liked both of them. She knew it had been a hard year for Hank since he'd lost India. She'd meant to stop by to see him once in a while and felt guilty that it had never happened. Time always got away from her. Tyne and Steph had been there for him, though. She reached over to pet Chester's head. "He's looking pretty happy."

Hank smiled. "He really missed India when she died, but he's adopted Sadie now. He runs to her place at least once a day."

Sadie nodded. "His favorite thing is when we're all together, though."

"It feels like family." Hank scratched behind the dog's ears.

Sadie finished her cheese dog and handed a French fry to Chester before looking at Miriam. "Has Grams hit you guys up yet for the church social on the Fourth of July?"

"That's less than three weeks away."

"Everyone's donating something." Hank tore off a little of his hot dog to feed Chester. "I'm baking cookies and Sadie's making different flavors of frozen custard to make ice cream sandwiches."

Miriam's eyes lit up. "I bought three of those last year. My favorite was the cherry custard between chocolate crinkle cookies."

Hank bent to scratch behind Chester's ears. "Those were Chester's favorites, too. Grams talked about asking Joel to donate plain hot dogs for the kids."

"I think he'd go for that."

Sadie gathered up their trash to throw away. "We'd better go. Steph's doing us a favor. We don't want to take advantage of her."

Miriam stood, too. "I'd better get back to work. I just came to pester you during my lunch break."

"Glad you did." Hank tugged on Chester's leash and led him to his truck.

When Miriam went back inside, she told Joel, "You'll be getting a phone call from Grams about her church social on the Fourth. If you're smart, you'll give her whatever she wants. She knows everyone in the entire area and all of them love her."

"You're telling me it's good business to keep Grams happy?"

"Pretty much."

Joel wrapped an arm around her waist. "I like spoiling the special women in my life."

Miriam gave him a quick kiss. "Good answer."

They spent the next hour getting ready for the supper rush. Just as she'd expected, they had plenty of business, but nothing they couldn't handle.

"We owe Harley a beer," Joel said.

"I'd throw in a free hot dog, too." Miriam went to grab Adele to leave the brewery a little early. "If you can make it, Tyne and Daphne invited us for supper tomorrow night."

Miles was just walking into the dining room and said, "Go. Sunday nights are probably slow. People have to go to work Monday mornings. I can cover for you here."

"Are you sure?" Joel really wanted to go; Miriam could tell.

Miles gave him a look. "Go. We'll be okay."

"If it's a madhouse tomorrow, we can change our plans, but thanks. I'll take you up on that."

The brothers were both looking awfully happy when Miriam and Adele left them. On the drive home, Miriam thought about how lucky Joel was that Miles had come to work for him. It was good for both men. And tonight, when Joel walked out the brewery's doors, he'd come to stay with her. Seven days a week. That was even better.

# Chapter 34

Joel didn't open the brewery until noon on Sunday. At two thirty Nick and Meg walked in, right after the lunch crowd had thinned out. He was happy to see them. He'd thought about Nick off and on. "Hey, how's the new job and the renovation?"

Nick looked at Meg and grinned. "It's going so well, we've gone in together to buy the rundown apartment complex on County Road."

The brewery was busy, but they weren't buried, so Joel sat down at their table. "The apartment complex? That's a little away from town, isn't it?"

"Not too bad." Today, instead of her usual jeans, Meg wore short shorts that showed off her long, tanned legs. A scooped neckline displayed her perky breasts. A good move, Joel decided, because Nick kept glancing at them. "The apartments are close to Harley's winery."

Joel remembered now. Halfway between the lake and the winery. A great location. "So you're going to become apartment owners?"

Nick shook his head. "Nope. We're going to convert the place into a motel."

"Brilliant." Tourists stopped in Mill Pond on their way to the national park and its lodges because there wasn't any place to stay in town besides Ian's resort. The people who stayed there rented rooms by the week, not just for a few days at a time. Joel guessed a motel would almost always be full.

Nick grinned. "We think it will be a great investment."

Joel had to agree. "Before we know it, Mill Pond will be even busier than it is now. How many rooms?" he asked.

"Ten, and there's an apartment off the office for the manager to live in." Nick looked at Meg. "We thought that would be a good incentive if someone wanted the job."

"How much work does it need?"

"A lot. The more we do, the better the sale price." Nick was talking specifics when Miles walked past the table, and Joel stopped him to introduce him to his friends.

Meg smiled at the two of them. "You look like brothers."

"Yeah, but I'm the good-looking one," Miles teased.

Meg nodded knowingly. "My sister Maddie always left me in her dust."

"Not anymore," Nick said, and Meg's eyes went wide. Nick grinned at her. "You've turned into one helluva looker, kid."

She blushed all the way to her hairline, and Miles motioned to the food counter. "Can I get you something?"

"We still haven't seen your menu and our lunch is on Joel." Nick tore off one of his free meal tickets and handed it to Miles. "We might have one of everything on the menu."

"Be my guest," Joel told him. "Besides the dogs, our sausages are really popular. Just spread the word how good our food is." Nick started to stand and Joel slapped him on the back. "Nice seeing you again." He went to help Collin in the bar. Miles drifted to the counter, and Nick and Meg went to place their orders.

The pace stayed steady through the afternoon until five o'clock drew near; then there was a small surge in business. By six things were getting quiet again.

Miles looked at Joel. "Go on. Get out of here. Have a nice supper with your friends."

"Thanks." Joel felt funny walking out of the building while the OPEN sign was still in the window, but Miles could handle the rest of the night. He went to pick up Miriam and Adele, then headed to Tyne and Daphne's. They reached their cabin by six thirty.

Daphne grinned when she opened the door for them. "I've lost my tenant. He's found better quarters to live in. Seems my best friend is stealing my renters."

Miriam snorted. "You already have a great roommate. You don't need mine."

She patted Joel on the head and Tyne called her on it. "That's the way Hank pats Chester. Joel's a guy, not a dog."

Joel lifted Miriam's arm and put it over his shoulder, making their height difference obvious. "She can touch me any way she wants to. I love it all."

Adele frowned, a little lost. "Miriam pets her cats. She doesn't pat them."

"That's because they don't drool over her," Tyne teased.

Adele smiled, but she'd smile at anything Tyne said to her. She was besotted with the man. If he showed a dimple, she would sign her life away.

Joel ignored him and sniffed the air. "Something smells good." Garlic and onions drifted toward him, along with wine and oregano.

"My lady picked the menu tonight—marsala chicken, mashed potatoes, and spinach salad with warm bacon dressing."

Adele pouted. "No dessert?"

Tyne's dimples showed and Adele blinked. Ian was handsome, Harley was good-looking, but Tyne was downright sexy. "Daphne watched *The Pioneer Woman* on the Food Network on Saturday mornings. We're having Ree Drummond's recipe for hot fudge chocolate cake."

Adele looked excited. So did Miriam, and Joel made a mental note to always have chocolate in the house. "Is there ice cream?" Adele asked.

"Yup, and maraschino cherries." Tyne gave Daphne a naughty glance. She raised an eyebrow at him and he didn't say anything else.

"So all right already." Miriam started for the kitchen. She and Daphne had been friends since grade school. "Are you going to feed us or not?"

Daphne laughed. "We thought we'd eat on the back porch. Tyne screened it in. No bugs. And it's beautiful outside."

"I brought a cooler full of beer," Joel said. "Want me to get it?"

"You get the drinks and I'll get the food." Tyne headed to the kitchen.

Joel went to the pickup and came back with an interesting assortment of bottles.

Ten minutes later they were sitting at a big, round table on the back porch. Tyne hadn't just screened it in, he'd made it into a three-season room. With the windows open, it felt almost like being outside, but without any rain or insects. Joel thought about Miriam's back patio. The lake was so beautiful, a room like this would make it livable a lot longer.

The food, as always, was droolworthy. Joel understood why Tyne made so much of it; people always wanted seconds. Every time Joel left this cabin, he'd probably gained five pounds. He told them about seeing Nick and Meg at the brewery and their plans for a motel.

"That's damn smart," Tyne said. "I swear, every time I turn around, more people come to Mill Pond."

"That won't affect your resort, though, will it?" Miriam asked. "You and Paula are already worked half to death."

Tyne shook his head. "We're full to the brim, but more people can't hurt us. The more people who come, the more who might want to book with us during the slow season. Ian's doing decadent specials for holidays during the winter months, but the resort's fun even when the weather's bad. Instead of outdoor activities, guests can enjoy being pampered when it's rainy or cold."

Miriam told them about her family's get-together this afternoon. She smiled. "Clair's tummy is beginning to poof out a little."

Tyne shook his head. "Kids. They're a big responsibility."

Joel glanced at Adele. "Yeah, but they're worth it."

His daughter smiled. Joel had always told her how lucky he was to have her. Miriam smiled, too, and Joel realized she was becoming almost as attached to Adele as he was.

Daphne had a big, goofy grin on her face when she looked at her old friend. "We're pretty damned lucky, aren't we?"

"You'd better know it." And Miriam's satisfied tone made Joel drown in happiness. It was like Mill Pond had been his ticket to good things. He was working with Miles, he was living with Miriam, and Adele was as happy as he'd ever seen her. What more could he ask for?

# Chapter 35

Miriam waved off Joel and Adele when they left for the brewery on Monday morning. Joel had insisted on taking Adele with him. "Sometimes it's nice to have a day completely to yourself. She's had a big weekend. She can chill in my office today."

Miriam had to admit the idea of being blissfully alone sounded like heaven. For starters, she carried a cup of coffee and a book to her chair overlooking the lake. Tommy and Tuppence followed her, happy to explore the yard. The usual duck paddled by, slowing a little to tease the cats because it was in deep-enough water. She watched the sunlight dance on the ripples of the water, let her mind drift, enjoying the moment, and then opened her book and submerged herself in its pages. By ten thirty, she started to get restless, so she went inside and surprised herself by looking through her cupboards and refrigerator for ingredients that might make a meal.

Sad news: There were none. Joel had promised to bring food home tonight so he wouldn't have to cook, but she felt as though most couples or families probably had more groceries in their kitchens than cans of soup, milk, bread, cereal, and three gallons of ice cream. She decided to remedy that.

She stripped the beds and started a load of laundry before she headed to Art's Grocery. When Art saw her with a grocery cart, he looked again and grinned. "I'm putting this on my calendar. I never thought the day would come."

"I'm making an effort here." She pointed to the long coolers filled with meat. "Do you still have any of those recipes Mary made for people who don't like to cook? Either that or I'm just going to grab anything that looks good and hope for the best."

"Give me a minute. I have some in my office. I still print them once in a while and put them out during tourist season." He disappeared for a minute and she studied different cuts of meat. Her mom loved to make ham steaks, so she put one of those in her cart. Her dad loved pork chops, so she added a package of those, too. She recognized the chuck roast. Tyne had cooked one of those in a slow cooker. Everyone liked hamburger, right? But there were three different kinds. Which one was which?

"Get the ground chuck," Art said, coming to hand her a small stack of papers. "Eighty percent meat and twenty percent fat for flavor."

She tossed two packages in her cart, then frowned at the variety of Mary's recipes. "I'm going to buy everything on these lists. Then I should be able to make all kinds of things, right?"

Art nodded. "Those are pretty foolproof, but you're going to be here a while. You've never visited half the aisles in this store."

She gave him her schoolteacher look, but he knew her too well. He just laughed at her and headed back to his office. "Good luck!"

Luck wasn't enough. It took her over an hour to find everything she needed. Then she had to check out, take the groceries home, and put them all away. No wonder she'd never cooked before. She remembered Joel telling her that Adele loved chicken breasts dipped in crushed potato chips, so she left one package of chicken in the refrigerator and put the other one in the freezer. Mary's recipe for spaghetti with meat sauce looked good to her, so she left the tube of Bob Evans bulk sausage in the fridge, too. Mary browned the sausage, then added frozen chopped onions and frozen diced green peppers. Sliced mushrooms were optional, according to a side note. When the vegetables were soft, she stirred in a big jar of spaghetti sauce and dropped the spaghetti in to boiling water. Miriam decided she could do that. Maybe.

When she had everything in its place and had taken out the laundry, she was too tired to fix herself more than a peanut butter sandwich. She carried that onto the back patio, downed it with a bottle of beer, then put on her gardening gloves and got to work. Tommy and Tuppence came to help her. They chased every bee and butterfly that flew past them.

She was working on her third bed when she glanced at her watch. Six o'clock. How the hell had that happened? She finished up and went in to take a shower. It was seven by the time she made the beds and carried a bowl of ice cream out to eat in her chair. She waved at a friend who went by in his boat. He and his wife had their grandkids staying with them this week. The kids waved from the backseat.

Miriam heard herself sigh. When had she started doing that? Was it a bad thing? She was too happy. Joel was easy to live with, to spend time with. She loved kids but had never wanted any of her own. Adele was nineteen, but she felt like a kid. Miriam enjoyed her. She'd never felt vulnerable before, but she did now. She understood how Daphne had felt when she'd thought she'd lost Tyne. Devastated.

What would she do if Joel and Adele moved out and moved on? She already knew the answer. She'd crumple, but she'd survive. But God, it would hurt.

She went into the house and sank onto one of the chairs by the fireplace. She opened her book, started reading, and the next thing she knew, she heard Joel's truck pull into the drive. She jerked awake. Her book had fallen onto the floor and she'd drooled a little when her head lolled to the side. Doggone!

She pushed to her feet and went to greet them, but she felt groggy. How long had she slept? She had no idea. Adele hugged her on her way inside, and then Joel hugged her next. He had two bags in his hands that smelled like sausage and tomato sauce. Her stomach growled.

"Sausage rolls." He shook his head. "You didn't eat anything, did you? You've been waiting for us."

"I'm starving." She didn't mince words. Food was an integral part of her life and Joel knew it.

He laughed and headed to the kitchen. "I'll get the paper plates." When he opened the refrigerator to grab a bottle of water for Adele, he froze. "There's food in here."

She'd come up behind him and smiled. "I went to Art's Grocery and stocked our kitchen today. I got recipes Adele and I can make, too."

"You even have eggs. I can make breakfast before I leave in the morning." He turned and pressed a hand to her forehead. "Is this the same girl I met at Chase's bar?"

"Don't be a smart-ass. It's no fun cooking for one person." She grimaced. "Who am I kidding? I'm never going to be a great cook, but I can feed us. And when you want something better, you can cook."

He pulled her close to hug her. "I love you just the way you are— no cooking skills required."

"How much do you love me?"

He blinked. "A lot."

"Then feed me."

He threw back his head and laughed.

*Very funny.* "Enough with the mushy talk, I'm hungry."

Chuckling, he carried the food and plates to her small kitchen table. She meant to be polite. She really did, but she ended up eating one of the sausage rolls all by herself. Joel and Adele shared the second one.

When they went to the living room and turned on the TV, Miriam had trouble staying awake again. Everyone looked tired. Finally, Adele said, "I'm going to my room to watch a little TV." She wouldn't last long. She was yawning as often as Miriam and Joel were. Joel did his best to stay awake, thinking Miriam would like some company, but for the first time ever, she looked at him and said, "I'm wiped out."

He pulled her to her feet and they called it a night. She couldn't even work up the energy for one good romp. They stripped out of their clothes and she collapsed onto the bed. Would he take that as lack of interest? Would it make him rethink things? But then he turned to her and spooned her against him. "I'm happy just holding you. I love you, Miriam."

Oh, how wonderful was this man? She fell asleep, feeling secure in his arms.

# Chapter 36

Joel could feel the excitement building for the Fourth of July. People in Mill Pond took their holidays seriously. His life had settled into a warm, fuzzy routine of happiness. He loved his work and he loved Miriam and Adele. Miles and he had found a pattern that made the brewery hum like the clichéd well-oiled machine. He'd hired enough people so he could take Sundays and Mondays off to spend time with Miriam, and Miles got Thursdays and Fridays off. His brother was beginning to meet people and become a part of the community. Joel offered to hire another cook so Dave could have a free day, too, but quickly gave up on that idea when he made it clear that work grounded him and he didn't want some interloper in his kitchen.

"But what if you get sick? Or need some time off?" Joel asked.

"You can worry about that when it happens. You and Miles both cook with me sometimes. You can manage."

Joel could cook everything on the menu if he had to. So could Miles, so they left it at that. Casey, Collin, Gia, and Kelly—Audrie's middle sister—made their own schedules for the bar and liked it that way, so he left them alone, too.

The Tuesday before the Fourth, business was slower than usual. It would be even slower on Wednesday; Chase's once-a-week barbecue was that popular. So when Joel, Miriam, and Miles milled around the counter for a short break, Dave came out to yak with them.

The Fourth was on a Thursday this year, and Joel was closing the brewery. Everyone would be at the cook-off at the lake. Last year Chase had sponsored it for suppliers and friends in the parking lot of his bar. The town council had liked the idea so much, they'd decided to make it an annual event, with everyone invited. It was a big deal. Chase and Paula—Chase's wife and Ian's chef at the resort—and

Tyne—her fellow chef, along with Tyne's hot-shot chef brother from California, would all man a grill at two in the afternoon to see who could make the best burger. Grams's church offered sides for three bucks—potato salad, baked beans, three-bean salad, and coleslaw, along with the cakes and pies the women carried in. All the money went for missions. Art donated tons of chips and people carted in melons and coolers filled with drinks.

Dave told Joel and Miles, "Last year Paula won. This year the rumor is that Tyne's gunning for her."

Joel smirked. "I think he has a chance, but lots of people say the hot-shot brother will have an advantage."

Dave studied him a minute. "You hardly ever smirk. You know something."

Dave was too damned astute. "Tyne helped me, so I owed him a favor."

"You're not going to tell."

"Not on purpose."

Dave grinned. "I like that. I respect it." He went on, "The brother's not being judged by fellow professionals. The people who line up for food vote. I gotta give it to them; they're fair. They vote for the burger they like best, not their friends, but fancy stuff doesn't go over that well. Last year Holden made lamb burgers. They might be popular in California, but most people here would rather have bacon and beef."

Miriam licked her lips. "That's my favorite." She batted her eyes at Joel. "How *did* you help Tyne?"

"Can't tell, not even you."

Dave tried to change the subject. "Bet they hit you up for hot dogs and sausages this year."

"I only supplied the dogs. Harley's in charge of that grill." He exchanged a knowing glance with Miriam. "I couldn't offer the sausages."

Her eyes went wide. "Oh, I get it."

"Too expensive?" Dave asked.

"Something like that."

Dave's grin looked like the Cheshire cat's. He turned his attention to Miles. "Are you going for the food?"

"What does a meal cost there?"

"Three bucks for sides and two for a plate of each slider, so you can sample them all. The town covers the rest of the expenses. The hot dogs are free. No Coneys; just ketchup, mustard, and onions or relish."

"Then count me in. I haven't had a hamburger for a while now."

"Do you go to Ralph's on your days off?" Joel had thought about having Miles over for a meal at Miriam's cabin, but whenever he had a day off, Miles worked.

Miles shrugged. "I usually just stay home and make something easy."

"Like frozen dinners?" Joel was hoping he'd say no.

"Maybe."

Joel shook his head. "Miriam and I need to get you to her place so I can grill for you."

"Yeah?" Dave raised his eyebrows. "What would you make?"

Joel heard the challenge and was ready for it. "Grilled pork chops with a Carolina honey glaze, topped with pineapple with a sweet rum sauce."

Dave laughed. "You must have a few special meals up your sleeve."

"Hey, I do better than that. I have at least five or six."

"If you invite me some time, we can trade off. I'll cook for you at my place."

Dave? Being social? "Why not? Maybe we can invite Tyne, too, and you two can talk chef talk."

Dave hesitated, then nodded. "Tyne's cool. I'd like that."

Customers started walking in then and they had to take their stations, but Joel had enjoyed their short time together. It made him look forward to the Fourth even more.

# Chapter 37

Joel suspected Mill Pond turned out en masse for every holiday of the year. When he looked up and down the lake's shoreline, people were milling everywhere. Ten grills were spaced along the public beach, two each per cook, and Miriam tugged on his arm to lead him to Tyne and Daphne. Miles was already helping Tyne slather buns with garlic-flavored butter and Dave was heating up a huge skillet of sliced onions and fennel, but they all smiled when they saw Joel. He was rolling a big cooler of his beers behind him.

"We're sitting with them tonight," Miriam told him. "They've already saved us spots."

"Have you claimed a spot?" Joel asked Dave and Miles.

"I'll probably mill around," Dave said. "I get antsy if I stay in one place too long."

Miles shrugged. "Not sure yet."

Joel paused to study him. His brother's voice had an edge to it. "Are you okay?"

"Why wouldn't I be?" Miles finished all the top buns and started on the bottoms. "It's a perfect day for this, right?"

Something was off, but Joel couldn't pinpoint it. If he made a big deal out of it, though, his brother wouldn't appreciate it, so he let it go. Adele stayed close behind Joel, slightly overwhelmed, but when people started waving to her, she relaxed, ready to have fun.

"Hey, come sit with us for a while," Hazel called to her. "You can catch me up on what you've been up to."

Adele glanced at Joel and he nodded for her to go. With a grin, she started off to see her friends.

Tyne was finishing setting up his work station, a long, lightweight portable table, when they reached him. He grinned, pointing to two big coolers. "Thanks for sharing your secret weapon with me, Joel. It's going to up my game."

Adele turned back to them and blinked. "Dad has a secret weapon?"

Miriam and Daphne exchanged conspiratorial glances. Daphne said, "David Danza makes a special sausage mix for your dad that customers love. Joel let Tyne add it to ground sirloin from Carl Gruber to come up with a perfect balance of lean and fat with a punch of flavor."

Joel laughed when Tyne lifted a cooler's lid to show him mountains of patties. "I knew this was a foodie town, but I'd never have guessed how seriously you guys take it."

Unimpressed, Adele left them, and Miles started putting patties on the first hot grill. Tyne started to fill the second. Joel looked down the beach and saw the other chefs were starting their burgers, too. The head of the city council picked up a microphone and announced, "The grills are going. The contest will start in fifteen minutes, when I blow my whistle. Eat and enjoy, and remember to vote for your favorite burger."

Dave and Tyne were flipping burgers and sipping beers. Tyne nodded down toward Harley at the opposite end of the shore, grilling dogs. "I promised him you'd bring him a beer. Chase and Paula, too. And my brother Holden."

It was a good thing Tyne had told him to bring extra. With a nod, Joel went to get the second, smaller cooler he'd brought and Miriam went with him to deliver them. Harley waved them to him. "I'm working up a thirst. Kathy here"—he motioned to his wife, a pretty woman with flowing blond hair and a heart-shaped face, who was grilling next to him—"brought her wine, but there's nothing like beer on the beach."

They stayed to talk with Harley and his family for a while. His dad and his new wife, Vicki, had brought two big picnic baskets filled with red and white wines and antipasti. They sat on a blanket, noshing, while Harley and Kathy grilled. Then they dragged the cooler down to Chase and Ian. They handed them each a cold bottle of brew and put four more on their worktable.

Miriam shook her head at Ian. "Why are you helping Chase when both your chefs are working their asses off?"

Ian grinned. "You answered your own question. Which of my

chefs would I choose? That's a no-win proposition, so I decided to avoid it." His two-year-old, Drew, ran to him while he talked, and Tessa had to run to scoop the boy up. She motioned toward their blanket, sprawled next to Chase and Paula's.

"If you get a chance, come to say hi to us when the feeding frenzy's over."

"Will do." Miriam nodded to Paula a few feet away. "We owe her a beer, too."

Joel glanced down the shoreline at Miles to check on him. His brother was smiling, but his expression was too bright, too fake. It was the smile Miles had used when he was younger, before he'd had to take a test he hadn't studied for. A worry wormed in Joel's gut. What was bothering Miles? Too many people? No, he was around them all the time at the brewery. Not enough structure? He was surrounded by partying and booze. Maybe too much temptation? He hadn't shown any interest in the beer at the microbrewery.

Steph caught his attention and waved at them. She was helping Paula. *No more time to brood.* Paula had trained Steph in the resort's kitchen before she went into bread making and catering with Hank.

Paula gave them a thumbs-up. "We're parched. Thanks."

Joel handed out beers and Paula arched an eyebrow at him. "You're at least going to try my burger before you vote for Tyne's, aren't you?"

"I've pledged to vote for my favorite."

"A man of scruples. Then I'm okay, because mine's the best."

Miriam laughed at her. "Have you played with your winning recipe?"

"Not much, but I had to tinker with it a little. The guys all know what I did last time and they'll try to top it."

Holden called down to them, "Talking about the guys, I'm parched down here, too, and my brother wouldn't share one of your brews with me."

Paula motioned for Joel and Miriam to give him the last of the beers. "Men from California whine a lot. You'd better pamper him."

Ralph was helping Holden, and he looked worried. "I've never cooked with a chef before," he said when Joel handed him a beer. "I feel like I need a meat thermometer so I don't screw it up."

Holden tipped back his beer and took a long swallow. "Good stuff, but I've watched Ralph in his diner. I've got a good partner."

Miriam glanced at a beautiful woman with sleek black hair and long, lean legs sitting on a blanket behind him. She looked as if she could be a model.

Holden nodded. "I brought JoJo with me this year. I'll introduce you at my victory celebration."

Miriam snorted. "I love your confidence."

The councilman stood and raised his whistle. Holden said, "Got to start plating these. See you later."

They pulled the empty cooler back to Tyne's grill. Miles put his head down and got busy, avoiding Joel. Tyne grinned at them. He looked scruffier than usual today, but that look worked for him. Hell, any look worked for him. "What's my competition like? What kinds of meat are they using?"

Miriam shook her head. "Calm down, Pretty Boy. We're not spies. You have to win fair and square."

He looked at Joel, and Joel would have told him, but the whistle sounded and people swarmed toward them. Joel had to admit Tyne's burger was delicious. He served it on a pretzel bun with a spinach/ artichoke sauce, a thin slice of tomato, and fried onion crisps on top. Everyone asked him about the blend of meat, but he told them it was a chef's secret.

Chase made his usual bacon cheeseburgers but added a ranch-style dressing topping, and Paula made a meat loaf mix burger with a ketchup glaze and mozzarella cheese. Holden went a tiny bit too fancy again with a ground half duck/half brisket burger with pickled red onions and brie. Joel loved it, but Tyne won, though it was really close.

When the contest was over and Tyne had received his small statue, people grouped together with friends to visit and relax. Miles trailed off with Dave. Joel and Miriam sat with Tyne and Daphne but went for frequent visits to see Harley and Chase and Paula. Holden and JoJo came to sit with Tyne.

At five, Grams's church hauled out homemade ice cream and sundae toppings for a donation. Miles wandered back to their blanket to eat with them. It was the perfect end for the day, and then, the minute the sun set, the fireworks started.

One minute Miles was sitting next to Joel and the next, when Joel turned to him, he was gone. Joel assumed he'd seen someone he knew and had gone to chat with them, or maybe Dave had called him over to introduce him to someone, but twenty minutes later he started to worry. By the end of the night, when the last fireworks drifted away as smoke, he started asking around for him. Dave came wandering back to them and said, "I watched him go to his truck and drive away right after the program started. Figured he didn't like fireworks."

He'd liked them as a kid. Joel tried to call Miles, but he didn't pick up. Something didn't feel right. Joel drove Miriam and Adele home and dropped them off, then went to check on his brother.

He pounded on the door of the trailer and Miles called, "It's open."

His voice was slurred. Joel braced himself before walking in. Miles was slumped on the couch with empty beer bottles scattered around him. He was holding a half-empty bottle of whiskey. Joel glanced at the beer—taken from the brewery. "Hey, Bro, you've had enough. Time to call it quits."

Miles shook his head. "Not drunk enough yet."

"You're plenty trashed. Sleep it off. You don't work tomorrow. You can sleep in." But once Miles started drinking, he usually didn't quit. At least, not for a while.

Miles stood and pointed to the door. "Just go. Leave me alone." He wobbled on his feet and then slumped back onto the sofa.

"Give me your key to the brewery." Joel held out his hand. "I don't want you to take any more beer." Miles could get more tomorrow, but they were closed tonight.

Miles pointed to his keys on the sink counter. "Go ahead. Take it."

Joel didn't want to, but he didn't *not* want to either. He didn't want Miles to spend all Friday drinking. One of his benders could last a few days. Then he glanced at the counter and his stomach sank. Two bottles of whiskey and a bottle of tequila waited there.

Miles grinned. "I stopped on my way home before the liquor store closed." He tipped the whiskey bottle to his lips.

Joel grabbed one of the bottles and tossed it in the trash.

"Don't!" Miles lurched to his feet and almost fell, trying to rescue his liquor. He pushed Joel away and stood between him and the counter. His face scrunched in anger. He'd throw a punch if Joel reached for the tequila.

Joel shouted, "Why now?" Confusion and frustration churned inside him. "You've been sober since you got here. Why ruin it now?"

Miles blinked, then shrugged. "Seemed like a good time."

Glib answers. Joel deserved more than that. His fingers itched to throw every bottle against the wall and smash it to bits. And then what? Would he and Miles wrestle each other and duke it out? Miles could go buy more of everything on Friday morning. Probably would. Well, to hell with him! Joel turned and stalked out the door. He stopped on the bottom step and yelled, "Will you be at work on Sunday?" That was the day Miles covered for him.

"Not sure," Miles said. "Hope so."

"I need to be able to count on you."

"Well, you can't, can you?"

"Forget it!" Joel snapped. "You're fired."

"Fine with me. Want your trailer key, too?"

"No. Someone has to take care of you." It was too much. Joel slammed the door and drove home, fuming the entire the way.

# Chapter 38

Miriam dropped Adele at the brewery early Friday morning. "Don't bother your dad. He's in a bad mood. Just go to the office and stay out of his way until he calms down."

Adele nodded, looking upset. "The last time Dad was mad was when Mom came and took me to visit a friend for three days without telling him."

"That would make anyone mad." Poor Joel; he must have been sick, worrying about her.

"He yelled at Mom. He never yells."

"We all get angry when someone scares us. Your dad didn't know if you were safe or not."

She frowned. "Is he scared now?"

How much to tell her? "He's worried about Miles."

Adele got a knowing look. "Miles drinks too much. Grandma said so."

"That can make you sick, and Miles might be sick now. Your dad loves his brother."

Adele smiled. "Dad loves lots of people. He loves you."

"I know, and I love him right back. And you, too."

Satisfied, Adele limped into the building and disappeared. Miriam drove to Miles's trailer. Joel didn't expect her to show up for work until eleven, so she had plenty of time to check on his brother. Joel had come home last night and told her everything. She couldn't believe he'd fired Miles, but he was too upset to discuss it. He hadn't come to bed with her but stalked outside and sat in the chair, overlooking the lake. She'd left him alone, giving him space to sort things out. She'd hoped they could discuss it more in the morning, but when she woke, he was already gone.

She gave a quick knock on the trailer's door, then turned the knob. It was open. She stuck her head inside. "Miles?"

No answer.

She let herself in. The TV was blaring and Miles was in his boxers, passed out, half on, half off the sofa. She grabbed the remote and turned off the noise. He didn't stir. Two empty whiskey bottles lay on the carpet. She walked into the kitchen and started a pot of strong coffee. When it finished brewing, she went to the couch. "Miles, wake up!"

He grunted and turned his head.

She reached down and shook his shoulder. "Get up! We need to talk."

He flinched and threw his hands over his head. "No, don't step there!"

Her heart hurt. He was reliving the day his friends in the military had stepped on the mine. And then she realized the fireworks had probably set off horrible memories for him. She pulled out her cell phone and dialed a friend, asked a few questions, and made a resolve. She went to shake Miles awake. "Get up! You need to get dressed."

He opened his eyes and blinked at her. "Go away."

"Not gonna happen. Get your sorry ass off this couch and come with me."

"I don't want to."

She shrugged. "Tyne has Fridays off and if I have to call him, I will, and we'll drag you out of here in your undershorts."

"Tyne?"

"Mr. Muscle and Attitude. He likes you. He'll be happy to help me get you in better shape."

"Not Tyne." Miles sat up and propped his head in his hands. "My head hurts."

"That's called a hangover. I made coffee." She went to get him a cup.

He made a face when he drank his first sip. "This tastes like shit."

"Ask me if I care. Drink up."

He finished the cup and handed it to her.

"Now water and aspirin." She brought those next.

He didn't look good when he finished them, but she didn't care about that either. "Get dressed. I'm driving you to my friend."

"What friend? Where are we going?" He headed back to the bedroom to find clothes.

"You're trying to fight a war alone that you're not going to win. You need help."

He stopped and leaned against the wall. "Our family doesn't ask for help. We fix our own problems."

"This one's too big for you. You're being a dumbass. Smart people know when they need help. It's a sign of strength to ask for it."

He shook his head. "Go away."

She opened her phone to punch more numbers.

"What are you doing?"

"Calling Tyne."

Miles held up a hand. "Stop. I'll go with you."

She closed her cell and put it away. "I haven't got all day."

"I'm going."

She heard him rummaging in the bedroom and he emerged five minutes later in jeans and a rumpled T-shirt. "Good, let's go."

He looked a little green around the gills, but he didn't get sick on the drive to Leticia Grayston's office. Leticia was the therapist Miriam had invited to speak to her high school students, the therapist who'd worked with the girl who'd tried to commit suicide last year. Miriam led Miles into her office and Leticia invited them both to take seats.

Leticia smiled at Miles. "Miriam says you're having a rough time of it since you heard the fireworks last night."

He shook his head and raked his hands through his hair. "They sounded too much like a battle. I had flashbacks. I used to dream about it all the time, but the dreams are going away, unless . . ."

"Something reminds you of those times." Leticia's voice was soft, soothing. "You're suffering PTSD, post-traumatic stress disorder. You've seen things you can't unsee."

His expression pinched shut, and Miriam leaned forward so he had to look at her. "It's like this. I love Joel and Joel loves you. So if you're not okay, he's not okay. You either get yourself together, or so help me, I'm going to kick your ass."

Miles stared at her, then smiled. "You mean it, don't you?"

"I don't make empty threats."

He nodded and turned to Leticia. "So what do I do now?"

Miriam left the office, letting them get to it. Miles was a wonderful person, and he was going to get better whether he wanted to or not. She'd see to that.

# Chapter 39

Joel looked out the brewery's windows and saw Miriam's car, parked at his brother's trailer. She'd called work to say she might be a little late today. It pissed him off, but she was a teacher. They couldn't help but try to fix everybody. He used to be like that, and then he'd married April. Enough said.

By the time she got to the brewery, customers were lined up for food and beer. Word had spread that Tyne had used Joel's sausage mix to help win the burger contest and they were selling sausage sandwiches as fast as they could make them. Joel kept waiting for a lull in business to talk to Miriam, but it never came. Tourists had flooded Mill Pond and the national forest for the Fourth and were making a long weekend of it. The brewery would probably be this busy again tomorrow. Hopefully, by Sunday, things would slow down.

Joel hadn't gotten much sleep last night. When he finally turned the sign in the doors to CLOSED, he was dragging. Miriam led Adele out of his office and waved at him. "I'll drive her home. She's been on her own most of the day, so we'll watch some TV while you finish up."

Usually, he appreciated her thoughtfulness. Tonight, it felt like she was avoiding him. He helped with cleanup, then went back to his office to stash the money and receipts in his safe. He'd run the numbers tomorrow morning. He couldn't concentrate tonight. On the drive home he wondered how things had gone with Miriam and Miles. She'd seen her load him into her old Mercedes and drive away. Where had she taken him?

When he walked into the cottage, she and Adele were watching *Dancing with the Stars*. They'd watched it on Monday night and recorded it, but Adele loved watching things over and over again. It was too freaking happy for him, so he grabbed a beer and went out to look over the lake.

A cloudless sky glittered with stars. The dark water lay smooth as a mirror. A frog croaked from the reeds by the channel. He felt himself relax. His eyes were just starting to close when Miriam called, "Adele's heading to bed. So am I. Are you tired?"

He roused himself and pushed to his feet. "I'm coming." He knew from experience that it wasn't wise to start a serious conversation when he was so tired, but he couldn't help himself. He closed the bedroom door behind him and said, "Where did you take Miles today?"

"To see my counselor friend. He has PTSD. The fireworks triggered flashbacks. She can help him." Miriam gave him a stern look. "He needs your help, Joel, not your judgment."

Ice flowed through his veins. "What do you know about me helping Miles? Do you know how many times I've bailed him out, helped pay his rent?"

Her shoulders squared. He'd used the wrong tone with her. He knew it, but she'd irritated him. Time and again he tried to be the good guy who rushed in to rescue people. Maybe he was getting tired of it. Her blue eyes snapped with temper. "I didn't know you were counting how many times he needed you. In my family when someone needs you, you show up."

"You don't have an alcoholic in your family, do you?"

"He wasn't an alcoholic until he joined the military."

"That was his choice, not mine."

Her hands went on her hips. "What? You didn't want him to join?"

"No, I didn't. It made us all worry about him. And guess what? It didn't turn out well."

"He could have died."

"Exactly, and we'd have been left grieving him."

She shook her head. "You've made this all about you. People have to do what's right for them."

"It was a bad choice."

"So was yours when you married April."

He jerked as if she'd slapped him. "So you're comparing me with Miles?"

"I'm just saying you both tried to make good choices, but they didn't turn out the way you expected."

"At least we tried. We didn't stay single and hide behind a desk."

It was her turn to gasp with surprise. "I wasn't hiding."

"If you say so."

She picked up his pillow and threw it at him. "I don't want to sleep next to you tonight." She opened the closet and tossed him a spare blanket. "The couch is comfortable."

"What's new?" He'd slept on the couch a lot when he was married to April. He yanked the door open, stalked through it, and slammed it shut.

He punched the pillow a few times before he burrowed into it. Lying there, staring at the ceiling, he came up with one idea after another. Daphne hadn't rented the apartment to anyone else yet. He could go back there. He could order a new trailer, too, and have it put on the opposite end of his property, by the brewery. He'd given the first trailer to Miles and wouldn't kick him out. He didn't want a homeless brother and he wouldn't send him back to live with their parents. His mind was still spinning when the bedroom door opened and Miriam came to him.

Her curls were mussed and she looked tired. "I can't go to sleep, mad at you."

This was new. April had wanted to spend as little time as possible with him. "I can't sleep either."

She held out a hand to him. "Come to bed with me?"

"When we're mad?"

"I still love you. We're not always going to agree. That's part of life, isn't it?"

He stood and pulled her to him. He hugged her so tight, he had to make himself loosen his hold. "Do you really think your friend can help Miles?"

"She's the best. She thinks she can, so I do, too, but I haven't fought this as many years as you have."

He followed her into the bedroom and slumped onto the mattress. "He's tried over and over again but just can't quit drinking."

She wrapped an arm around his shoulders. "Because he can't do it alone. He needs help. If he had diabetes, you'd take him to a doctor, wouldn't you?"

He rubbed his eyes, confused and tired. He took a deep breath. "I've hung in there this long. Why not stick it out a little longer?"

She kissed his cheek. "You're a wonderful man."

He didn't feel wonderful. He didn't even feel hopeful, but if something might help his brother, why not try it? "I'll stop in to see him before work tomorrow."

She lifted the covers and pulled him next to her. "I can sleep now."

He wasn't sure if he'd be able to, but with Miriam curled close to him a lot of his anxiety drained away and he drifted into slumber.

# Chapter 40

When Miriam walked into the brewery on Saturday, Miles was working. He looked like shit—dark circles under his eyes, pale complexion, and limp hair—but he was keeping busy. Miriam quirked her hands in the air in a question. "You're not on the schedule today."

He glanced at her, uncomfortable. "I know, but I needed to get out of the trailer. I need to keep my mind off things."

Joel walked into the dining room with the cash drawer to start the day. He looked at Miles and said, "Dave needs you for a minute in the kitchen, if you have time."

With a nod, Miles went to help him. Joel gave Audrie the drawer and then went to help Miriam finish wrapping the silverware. In a quiet voice, he said, "Dave wants to sponsor Miles. He's an ex-alcoholic."

"Dave? There's no such thing as an ex-alcoholic, just a recovering one."

"Well, he hasn't had a drink in a long time. That's why he left Miami—too much partying—drinking and drugs. That's why he likes small kitchens these days instead of prestigious ones. He's been sober seven years. Said he wouldn't have made it without his sponsor. Recognized Miles's drinking problem the same day he met him."

Miriam nodded. "There are probably signs."

"That's what Dave said. Anyway, if Dave helps Miles with his drinking and your friend helps him with his PTSD, Miles might make it this time. Dave said not to expect too much too soon, that he might slip a couple of times before he gets it right, but there's light at the end of the tunnel."

"That's wonderful." She added the last roll of silverware to the pile, then turned to press both of her hands to Joel's face. "I'm so proud of you. You try so hard to do the right thing."

"You gave me a not-so-gentle nudge in the right direction."

She wrapped her arms around him and kissed him hard. "You don't realize how special you are."

Audrie cleared her throat. "Better break it up, lovebirds. It's time to open the doors for business."

Miriam looked up. She'd lost track of time, and a long line had already formed outside. People were peering in at them, and Grams and Miguel were near the front. Grams had a huge smile on her face. Oh boy; their kiss would spread all over town.

Joel opened the doors and people moved to the counters. Miguel went to order their food and Grams hurried to Miriam. "Are you two going to make it official? You sure seem to like each other."

Miriam gave a naughty smile. "When are you and Miguel going to walk down the aisle?"

But it was impossible to fluster Grams. "We were both married and widowed. For now"—she winked—"we'd rather live in sin."

"I want more than that for Miriam," Joel said, coming to join them. "I'm nuts about the woman. I want to make her my wife."

Miriam turned to him, her eyes wide. "You want to marry me?"

"I'd put a ring on your finger right now if you'd let me. I want to make you mine."

"But I'm tall and geeky and gawky and . . ."

He shut her up with a kiss. "And wonderful. Marry me, woman."

"Yes!"

Grams looked like she'd won the lottery. "When will you have a date?"

"The sooner the better," Joel said.

"Will there be a barbecue?"

"What?" Joel blinked, caught off guard. "A barbecue? That's a new one."

Miriam gave him an indulgent grin. "In Mill Pond when a foodie couple marries, there's a barbecue on the beach and the whole town celebrates."

Joel chuckled. "Is there *anything* you don't celebrate on the beach?"

Grams shrugged. "Nothing that matters."

"In winter?"

"Well, that's different. Then we do a carry-in." Grams smiled.

She meant it, Lord help them. Oh, well, when in Rome . . . Joel threw up his hands in surrender. "Then why not?"

People cheered, and then business got back to usual. But it was official. Miriam had promised to marry him. Joel had come to Mill Pond and hit the jackpot.

# Chapter 41

The wedding took place two weeks later, and that was still too long for Joel. Miriam had said yes. He wanted to make it official. Everyone came. Miriam had warned him, but people rolled into wedding mode so fast, Mill Pond had to have a lot of practice at it.

Tyne and Chase made a lot of smoked briskets and chickens. Joel and Miles made tons of hot dogs and sausages. They had the reception at the brewery, and there was so much property, they put up volleyball nets, croquet games, and basketball hoops. People came and spent the day. Joel's parents came and took Adele home with them for a week. Miles and Dave made sides, like macaroni and cheese, broccoli salad, and German potato salad. Ian's wife, Tessa, made the wedding cake, and Mill Pond women carried in more desserts. Harley donated two crates of wine and Joel provided plenty of beer.

In the early evening a DJ spun music in the parking lot and people stayed to dance. Joel had a great time, but Miriam enjoyed it even more. By the time the music stopped and people cleared out to go home, they looked at each other. They had the cottage to themselves. Joel took two days off from the brewery for their honeymoon. Miles and Dave waved them off. "There's not much left for cleanup. Get out of here."

They drove to Miriam's cottage, and even though Joel had been spending every night there, it felt different. They were married.

Miriam locked the doors and started dropping her clothes on her way to the bedroom. "I'll arm wrestle you for who makes breakfast tomorrow morning."

"Breakfast?" Joel shook his head. "Maybe brunch."

She grinned. "I'm strong for a woman."

Joel let her win and she grimaced at him. "You lost on purpose."

"That's better than eating whatever you come up with for eggs."

She laughed. "Let's build up an appetite." And the woman meant it. The minute he dropped his drawers, she was on top of him.

"Hey, I'm not a bronco! Take it a little easy."

She shook her head. "I've always wanted to be a cowgirl. I'm going to ride you until you're done in."

He grinned. He had more stamina than she thought. Miriam was in for one hell of a ride.

## ABOUT THE AUTHOR

**Judi Lynn** received a master's degree from Indiana University in elementary education after attending the IPFW campus. She taught for six years before having her two daughters. She loves gardening, cooking, and trying new recipes. Readers can visit her website at www.judithpostswritingmusings.com and her blog writingmusings.com.

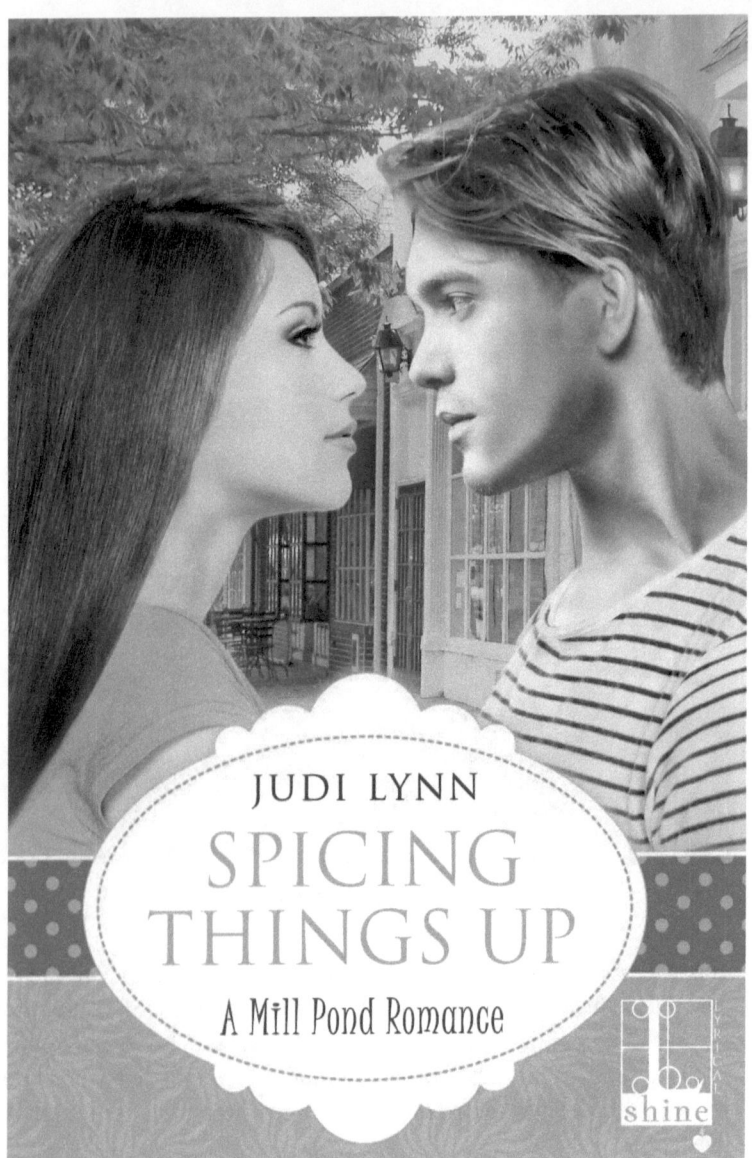

JUDI LYNN

# SPICING
# THINGS UP

A Mill Pond Romance